# MIA AND THE CURSE OF CAMELOT

Written by Rehannah Mian

Illustrated by Radu Secareanu

Cover art by Jake Smith

Copyright © 2021 Rehannah Mian

All rights reserved. No portion of this book may be reproduced in any form without permission from the publisher, except as permitted by U.S. copyright law.

*Camelot: The year 634*

*Morgana flew over the castle, turning the hearts of her terrified enemies to stone. Somewhere in the darkness a knight ran for his life as fire and lightning crashed down around him. Reaching the safety of the forest, he paused, opened his hands, and allowed a strange wind to carry the sealed letter through the air, towards the dungeon of the castle.*

# 1


## STICKNEY PYGOTT


*Somewhere there's a tree with a bookcase inside.*
*It will take you to the place where the forgotten people hide.*


Mia was twelve and alone again. She stared out the window of the care home and watched the mist dance around the twisted oak tree on the playing field. Its ancient branches formed a sinister black silhouette against the orange sky, but otherwise gave no clue to the secret it possessed. This was the fifth day in a row that she had woken at sunrise, waiting for the tree to glow again but as the mist drifted away, letting in the first pale blue of the morning, her hope faded. She sighed.

The bed looked cosy, and she was just thinking about crawling back in when something made her take one last look out of the window. She jumped for joy.

There it was! Brilliant white shards of light, exploding from the oak tree's bark.

Punching the air, she grabbed her backpack and tore down the stairs, tripping over her shoelaces as she went, but there was no time for her to stop and tie them as the tree's magic would only last a few minutes. Running from the house she sprinted across the playing field, narrowly avoiding Mr Oliver who was walking his dog, Cairo. Luckily, he was facing the other way otherwise he would have probably stopped her to comment on how unusually quiet it was, or to explain how much better it was in his day when there was not so much traffic about.

'I wish that I could go back to the old days,' he would say before shuffling away.

Mia kept running, her eyes firmly fixed on the oak tree. She felt bad because she liked Mr Oliver, but the tree's fiery flares were becoming paler. The magic was vanishing. She desperately grabbed at the last trails of flickering light as they disappeared into the bark, but it was no use. The final glimmer of magic had evaporated. Her heart sank and she slumped against the tree that had abandoned her to yet another lonely, boring day.

From the moment she had been 'dumped' at the care home, Mia had found comfort in the pages of her adventure books, longing to be part of something wild and exciting too, but she never really believed that it would happen to someone like her – until the day she met Stickney Pygott. *That* day, everything changed.

Her thoughts were broken when a solitary beam of light whizzed around the tree and hit her on the back of the head.

'OUCH!' she cried, turning round in annoyance.

The luminous corkscrew flew into a small hole in the bark above her head. Mia peered in after it, and her eyes widened.

'You're still here!' she croaked with teary relief. There it was - the carved bookcase inside the hollow, throbbing beneath a ghostly spotlight. She pushed firmly against the trunk of the tree, and with a low creaking noise the tiny hole began to grow, bigger, and bigger, until it was wide enough for her to step inside.

She walked over to the bookcase. It was filled with dusty parchments and old books of all shapes and sizes. A particularly large book with a gold cover caught her eye. Picking it up, she brushed away the dirt, revealing the name SIR MORIEN, written in dark ink down the spine. Inside the cover was a portrait of a dark-skinned man dressed in armour. Below it were the words, *Sir Morien, Fierce Knight of Camelot.*

Other than that, the pages were blank. Mia had read about Camelot in her adventure books. She remembered King Arthur, his magician Merlin, Morgana the witch, and a knight called Sir Lancelot, but she had never heard of Sir Morien.

Deciding that she wanted to meet him, Mia flipped the blank pages of the book until the magic words appeared. Then she read them out loud.


*'Magic oak tree, hear this rhyme,*

*take me travelling back in time,*

*where brave knights and dragons, and creatures of old*

*do battle for honour... and barrels of gold.'*

Blinding flashes filled the dark space, as though the sun were bouncing off the swords of a hundred fighting soldiers. Mia covered her eyes. The earth beneath her began to tremble as the roots of the tree spiralled up from the ground, forming a leafy staircase that disappeared into the chamber above. The ground eventually calmed, and the spotlight that had been shining down on the bookcase slowly turned and illuminated the stairway.

Mia dropped the heavy book on the floor and raced to the top. She climbed out onto the lowest branches and looked down upon the narrow winding streets and their crooked houses. A few early risers were out and about, and as she sat and tied her shoelaces, she noticed that Cairo had his eyes fixed firmly on the door of the newsagents, waiting for Mr Oliver to come out. She giggled. Cairo would probably be sitting there for a long time. Mr Oliver *did* like to stand and chat.

'It's so peaceful up here, Stickney' she said, leaning over the edge of the tree. 'I wish that I could live in your branches forever.'

Two gigantic eyes looked up at her and blinked.

'Oh, you made me jump,' stuttered the tree. 'Good morning, Mia. It's nice to see you again.'

Stickney Pygott stretched out his leafy arms and shook them awake, almost catapulting Mia to the ground. At almost eight hundred years old, he was the last living member of the Pygott oak tree family. He remembered when the town was filled with his relatives, and he did miss them terribly, but his roots still held all the memories he had collected over the centuries, and so whenever he was lonely, he would fall asleep and revisit those happy days through his dreams.

But whenever he was awake, he would pass the time watching humans come and go. He wished that they would stop occasionally so that he could tell them about all the important people that he had met since he was a sapling, but they never did. They always seemed so busy. Mia was different though, she would often strike up a conversation with him, which is why he trusted her with his secret.

'Well, I suppose we'd better get going while it's still quiet,' he said, wiggling the bottom of his trunk. 'Hold on now.'

Mia just managed to grab hold of a clump of leaves before Stickney turned on his engine and began to rumble. A moment later he leapt into the air, ripping his roots from the soil, and leaving a great gaping hole in the ground. They rocketed towards the sky, showering the startled townsfolk with clumps of worm-filled mud as his long trailing root-legs whipped back and forth, propelling them higher. Mia whooped for joy and spread out her arms as they soared over the town and then disappeared into the clouds.

'Get your brollyo ready!' shouted Stickney, tapping her on the back.

Brollyo? What's a brollyo? she cried, but by then they had entered a solitary white cloud that had a spectacular waterfall hidden inside it. They flew through the spray, soaking Mia through.

'Careful,' she cried, wiping the stinging water from
her eyes.

Stickney let the waterfall carry them down
through the cloud, paddling with his smaller branches
to keep them upright. Mia watched in awe as the foam

at the bottom of the cascade turned into fluffy white clouds that drifted off into the sky.

They glided peacefully along a mist-covered river at the bottom of the waterfall for a while, until Mia noticed that the water was starting to get rough and choppy. Stickney was struggling to stay balanced. The ripples became more violent, and Mia suddenly became aware of a distant rumbling noise, getting louder and louder. She looked down through the leaves and took a sharp intake of breath. The foamy water below was turning into rapids, and Mia could see the panic in Stickney's eyes.

'What's happening?' she cried, but Stickney remained silent, trying desperately to stop them capsizing.

Then she saw it. A second waterfall. They were heading straight towards it. Mia screamed for Stickney to stop but it was too late. *Fwooosh!* Over the edge they plummeted, and Mia felt herself free falling through the air.

A few seconds later she felt a branch wrapping itself around her. She held onto it for dear life.

'It's okay,' Stickney reassured her. 'You're quite safe.'

Before she knew it, they were at the bottom of the waterfall and tumbling out of the cloud. Stickney straightened himself up as if nothing had happened, and they continued on.

Mia was looking around, struggling to catch her breath, when she noticed the unusual colour of the sky. It was crimson red, and it had grey clouds that were steaming, as though they were boiling. The air smelt rancid like rotten eggs, which made her sneeze and cough, and she had to clamp her hand over her mouth to stop herself being sick. Suddenly, a thunderous cry filled the air and a ball of flames hurtled over her head. Stickney ducked to try and dodge it.

'Ouch!' he yelled as the fire set alight some of his leaves.

Mia prayed for dear life as a colossal dragon began to circle them. She curled herself into a ball after seeing the ridge of deadly thorns on its back.

With a thrash of its tail, the enormous, wide-headed creature torpedoed through the sky towards them.

'It's going to eat us!' she screamed, barely audible, feeling the dragon's meaty, charcoally breath in her face. But to her relief, it merely sniffed her with its cavernous nostrils, snorted a stream of warm snotty air into her face, and then flew away.

Mia sat rigid with fear as they flew on through the dragon realm, heading towards the bluer skies up ahead. Eventually, she fell asleep, and only woke when she felt them descending. She looked down, hoping beyond hope to see the playing field back home beneath them, but instead, she saw that they were heading towards a dark and haunted looking castle.

2

# THE MORBID MUSEUM

*Deep down in a dungeon, our ancestors dwell*
*in a dark tiled hall, where in battle they fell.*


Stickney Pygott flew down over the castle, casting a long dark shadow that made the grey towers and stone walls look even more bleak and depressing. He landed with a thud on an overgrown patch of grass next to the gatehouse and lowered a branch so that Mia could climb down.

'Where… are we?' she asked, gazing up at the grim fortress towering above her. It stood on a steep sided hill, making it even more threatening.

'What a miserable looking place. It looks full of secrets,' she mouthed quietly to herself.

A rustling sound caught her attention. It was Stickney, shaking his leaves, and not taking a blind bit of notice of Mia. He was furious that the dragon had scorched his leaves and was busy picking the ruined ones off with his long, twig-like fingers.

'Those awful mountain dragons!' he huffed. 'They have no manners at all… never have had!'

'Where are we?' repeated Mia, a bit louder this time.

'Camelot of course!' he answered, firmly. 'This is where you asked to come wasn't it? Where there are knights… and *dragons*. Well, I hope so because I'm not going back now. Not until I've recovered.'

Stickney continued to mutter to himself, but Mia instantly cheered up. She had made it to Camelot! She was just about to run up to the castle to look for King Arthur and Sir Morien, when she noticed that the drawbridge was raised, and that there were no guards in sight. The moat around the castle was dried up and full of weeds. She listened. Apart from Stickney shuffling around, the whole place was silent - eerily silent, as though it had been abandoned. Surrounding them was a dense forest, and knowing that Stickney was not in the mood to answer any more questions, Mia climbed the castle hill to see what was beyond it.

In one direction, the path led towards a jagged mountain range, which did not look inviting at all, but in every other direction was the even less-inviting forest, half covered by a weird, creeping fog. She decided that she had had enough adventures for one day, and that she was going to plead with Stickney to take her home. But as she looked back down the hill, she saw him stomping off into the forest.

'Come back, Stickney!' she called. 'Where are you going?'

She bounded down the hill after him. For a hulking great oak tree, Stickney Pygott could certainly move quickly. Mia struggled to catch up with him. She saw him walk up to a group of trees, angrily boot a few thistles out of the way with his foot, and shuffle his bottom into the soil. With a low drilling sound, he sunk his roots far down into the earth and became still. Mia was exhausted by the time she reached him, and she slumped forward with defeat when she saw his face vanish into the bark.

'Wake up!' she shouted, knocking on his trunk. 'I want to go home.'

But there was no response. Stickney Pygott was an ordinary, non-magical oak tree once more, and there he sat, just like any other tree, leaving Mia feeling alone, and very scared.

Now, oak trees are very good at picking up warnings, and if Stickney Pygott had *not* been sulking, he might have noticed the shadowy hooded figure that was standing by the castle, silently staring at Mia.

And if he had *not* been sulking, he might have been able to warn her to run! But no such warning came for Mia. She turned round to see the dark mass rising up in front of her. She watched in terror as it hovered above the ground, and then began to spin - slowly at first, then faster and faster until it became a black whirlwind, catapulting swirling black orbs of vapour into the sky. As they were released, each orb magically transformed into a shrieking black crow, which then flew at her.

Mia fled, running faster than she had ever run before as the birds closed in on her. She felt the snapping of their beaks on her clothes and hair as she dived into the dried-up moat and scrambled down into a large fox burrow. Mia looked out and saw the phantom crows circle the moat three times before finally flying off over the moatains.

On closer inspection, she saw that the burrow was in fact a tunnel, carved into the rock on which the castle stood. It was too dark to see all the way down but luckily, Mia always carried a torch in her bag. Her scout leader had once said that '*You never know when you might need one!*' And it turned out that he was right, although she was sure that he had *not* foreseen her running from a flock of demonic crows when he had said it! She switched it on and made her way down the gloomy passage.

It led her deep under the castle, through storage areas filled with barrels of food and wine. This brought comfort to Mia, as presumably the kitchens and servant's quarters must have been nearby. But as far as she walked, she never found any rooms or people. Deeper underground she went, trailing her fingers along the damp slimy walls as the tunnel became narrower and mouldier. The torchlight began to flicker. Mia gripped it tightly, praying that the battery would hold out.

Eventually, the tunnel opened out into a large chamber, with twelve great rock pillars supporting the roof. It would have looked like a prison dungeon if it were not for the elegant black and white tiles on the floor, and the freaky old statues and tombs all over the place. After shining her torch around to check that no one was hiding in the shadows, Mia wrapped her arms tightly around her stomach and slowly moved inside.

Making her way through the large collection of carved figures, she glanced uncomfortably from side to side, half expecting them to come alive at any moment. Up ahead she could see kings, queens, servants, and knights with their arms raised in front of their faces, and others that looked like they had been frozen solid while running from something. Scattered among them were marble dragons up on plinths, with their wings outstretched and their claws ready to attack. Small swordbearing gnomes stood guard along the walkways. The whole place looked like some grisly battle scene.

She shuddered and carried on, hoping to find a way into the castle. The torchlight picked up a knight, rearing on his horse and swinging a mace over his head. That one had been positioned to look like he was attacking a cowering king.

But it was the statue of a man in long robes that interested Mia the most. He had a magnificent knee-length beard, which someone had taken the time to carve with fine detail. He was wearing some sort of wizard's or magician's hat, and his mouth was wide open as though he was chanting a spell. Above his head, he held a large staff. She looked for any names carved into the tombs, but they had been worn or scraped away.

At the back of the hall, she noticed a large wooden door, barely visible in the dim light. It had a rusty metal handle, which she turned, but it was locked. Mia desperately tried to push it open with her shoulder, but it would not move. Standing on tiptoes, she shone her torch through the barred window at the top. There was another dark passage on the other side, but she could not see where it led, although she was convinced that she *could* see something shadowy moving down the passage towards her. Her trembling fingers covered her mouth, and she turned to run, but before she had taken more than a couple of steps, a hundred ghostly whispers filled the hall.

3

# THE GLOOMY LETTER

*A long time ago a witch travelled this land,*
*cursing her foes with a wave of her hand.*


'Go away!' Mia screamed, frantically whipping the torchlight from wall to wall to find the exit tunnel. The whispers went on, then were joined by a hollow, echoey sobbing. They seemed to be coming from every part of the room. One moment they were in her face, and the next, over her shoulder. Mia placed her hands over her ears to block them out. When the sounds suddenly stopped, Mia felt something move behind her. Quivering, she spun around but there was nothing there – at least nothing that she could see. She lifted her torch. The statues were still in their places - thank goodness. She had just let go of her breath when the sobbing noise appeared again. Only this time it was more mournful and snivelling, and it was at the far side of the hall.

'I'm gone!' she panicked, running towards the exit.

A few steps into the tunnel, something made her stop. What if there was someone trapped down there? She poked her head back out, keeping the rest of her body safely tucked away.

'Hello?' she called out, clearing her throat. 'Is…is anyone there?'

There was no answer. She crept forward, moving slowly towards the sound. A second noise appeared - a faint *drip drip,* which was getting louder with every step she took. She was doing her best to be brave, when the annoying voices in her head arrived – right on cue, as usual.

*What if there's a ghost waiting for you?* They hissed.

'Oh, stop it!' Mia cried, determined not to listen this time.

But on and on they went, saying things like, *what if the tunnel closes, leaving you trapped down here forever?*

They only disappeared when she reached the statue of the wizard, and her attention was drawn to the eerie orange light that was now illuminating it. The sobbing noise was coming from behind it. Nervously craning her neck to the side, she was able to see that the distraught soul was actually an old-fashioned parchment, floating in mid-air, and crying pitifully. Invisible hands were holding it open, and there was a small grey raincloud hovering above it, soaking it through.

Mia carefully approached it, accidentally stepping into the large pool of water that had formed on the floor. Shaking her foot and the parchment dry, she began to read what was written on it. It was a letter.

*Merlin,*

*We beg for your help. The witch, Morgana has cursed Camelot and turned King Arthur and his people to stone. She has locked them up in a dungeon below the castle, sealed with a spell, and she has taken the throne.*

Mia turned and looked at the statues. 'Cursed?' she panicked, realising that they were real people, and knowing that Morgana, the most terrifying witch she had ever read about, was somewhere nearby. She continued reading.

*We, the knights of King Arthur's Round Table, tried to stop her, but our swords and weapons were no match for her battle dragons and dark magic.*

*I am the only one of the Order who escaped, but I am now alone and unable to fight her on my own. I need your help, Merlin. I pray that this letter finds you. I await your help.*

The signature was from a familiar name.

'SIR MORIEN!' she exclaimed.

A feeling of dread suddenly washed over her, and she went to look at the face of the wizard again.

'Merlin!' she cried. 'No!'

There he was, this once great wizard, now nothing more than an ornament in Morgana's morbid museum.

As soon as Mia said his name, the letter began to wail loudly, and the little cloud began to flash with lightning. A thunderstorm was soon powering through the hall, so Mia pulled the soggy letter from the air, and sprinting towards the exit tunnel, she shouted to the statues, 'Don't worry. I will find Sir Morien and bring help!'

She did not notice the raincloud following her out.

4

# ODD JOB

*In the forest you'll find a warm gentle breeze*
*that whistles and dances through magical trees.*


At last, the darkness of the tunnel gave way to daylight, and Mia scrambled out. Her relief was quickly replaced with wonder when she saw that she was no longer in front of the castle where she had gone in, but instead, she was in the middle of a dark foggy forest.

She squeezed the water from her clothes, wondering whether she had accidentally come down a second tunnel in the darkness. But after some moments she decided that it *was* the same one, and that it had mysteriously changed direction. There was no sign of Stickney Pygott, and none of the other oaks looked familiar. Mia had no idea where she was, or what the noises were that were coming from the trees.

She was beginning to panic that Camelot might never let her go.

A warm breeze made her feel more hopeful. The mist was beginning to lift now, and when a golden blade of sunlight pierced the leafy canopy, Mia headed cheerfully towards it. A sudden movement next to her made her jump. She was surprised to see that it was the miniature raincloud, bobbing around Sir Morien's damp letter, which she was holding in her hand. Somewhere along the way, the cloud had stopped raining, and was looking much brighter. It even had a small rainbow arching over it.

Mia laid Sir Morien's the letter on the ground to dry, and smiled when the cloud sat beside it faithfully, but then the fluffy mass began to droop. It looked sad.

'What's the matter?' she asked, gently patting it on the head. It reminded her of a poodle. 'Do you belong to Sir Morien too? It's okay, we'll find him.'

The cloud whizzed around excitedly, making Mia laugh. When she and the letter were dry, she picked it up and put it in her backpack, and then she set off to find a path to follow. It soon became obvious that there was no easy way through the forest, and whichever way Mia went, there was an assault course of sharp brambles and fallen trees to climb over. She eventually came across a clearing that sloped down towards a river, and stopped to bathe her scratched arms.

She watched the fast-flowing water carry fallen leaves downstream, and she fished out a red, jagged-edged one that washed up next to her. It glistened in the sunlight, as though it had a coat of glitter. Mia rubbed it with her fingers, revealing the natural green colour underneath. It *was* glitter covering it – red glittery paint! She quickly filled up her water bottle and got to her feet.

'Come on!' she shouted to the cloud, which was playing happily in the river, and soaking up the spray of the water. 'We've got to go.'

They followed the river upstream, until some way on Mia noticed that the light in the forest was beginning to change, from earthy green to a sort of red - as though the sun was setting, but it felt different. She looked up and saw that the trees were covered with a blanket of the same unnatural - and quite unnerving - glittery red leaves that she had found by the river. Suddenly, something dropped from the sky and splattered by her feet. Mia looked down and saw a large blob of red sparkling paint soaking into the mud. A moment later a second, slightly smaller glob joined it.

She looked way up into the branches and saw the feet of a man tiptoeing hazardously on the top of a shaky wooden ladder. He was wearing a pair of long, knee-length brown socks - one of which, had fallen around his pointed cloth shoes, revealing one of the two scrawny legs that were poking from the bottom of his dark red tunic. He was busying himself, carelessly slapping a paintbrush back and forth over the leaves, while the gooey liquid poured down his arm.

'Is he… doing what I *think* he's doing?' Mia whispered.

The cloud floated up to the top of the tree then floated back down again. It nodded.

'That is so weird!' she said, 'Is he crazy?'

Another *splodge* of paint fell from above. Mia quickly stepped back to dodge it.

'Careful!' she shouted up.

The man jumped and bashed his head on a branch, letting out a cry.

'O-oh!' he sputtered, rubbing his head.

Then he saw Mia looking up at him.

'Good day to you!' he said, and began climbing down the ladder

The man was peculiar looking, with a billowing white beard, and scruffy hair that looked like two large bushes growing from either side of his head. The thick round spectacles perched on the end of his nose were two metal circles, joined in the middle by a small pin.

'I don't get to see many people anymore,' he said, then he checked around him, and lowered his voice to a whisper. 'Everyone I know has been turned to st...'

He came to an abrupt halt halfway down.

'Goodness!' he cried, gawping at Mia's clothes. 'Who might you be?'

Mia introduced herself to the man, taking great care to *not* mention that she had travelled through time. She had remembered reading that medieval people had a bad habit of using magical folk as bonfire fuel!

He then noticed the cloud floating above Mia's backpack. 'H-how did you find that?' he shuddered. 'D-did the witch send you?'

Mia was puzzled. 'I found it in a room full of cursed statues,' she explained, taking Sir Morien's letter from her bag, and showing it to him. 'It was hanging around this letter from Sir Morien, one of King Arthur's knights. Do you know him?'

'Sir Morien?' he exclaimed. His face brightened at the mention of the knight's name.

'Yes, I know him well.'

Mia was surprised that he had ignored the part about the cursed statues! He tossed his paintbrush into an old pot which was dangling from a branch, and jumped the last few rungs to the ground.

'But you won't find him around here,' he added. 'He fled during the battle of the interworlds.'

The smile dropped from the man's face, and he looked behind him once more to check that no-one was listening, then he lowered his voice again.

'When Morgana, the witch, defeated the knights, she turned everyone in Camelot into stone. I hid on the castle roof and watched Sir Morien escape into the forest on his horse, but I haven't seen him since. There is only me left now… and *her* of course.'

'And, who *are* you?' enquired Mia.

The man's smile returned, and he bowed.

'Oh, excuse me, Miss. My name is Job, but most people call me *Odd* Job because there isn't anything that I can't turn my hand to ... at least, I think that's why they call me that!' he added thoughtfully. 'I'm the castle caretaker…well, I *was* before the battle.'

He took a cloth from his pocket and wiped the paint from his fingers as he let his mind wander.

'The castle used to be so beautiful inside,' he recalled. The walls were painted gold and red, and the windows were draped with silk fabrics. And there wasn't a day went by when the great hall wasn't filled with people and laughter… but when the witch took the throne, I was forced to abandon my duties and wait on her like a slave.'

'Please tell me about the interworlds,' said Mia. 'And about what happened to Camelot.'

Job made himself comfortable on a tree stump.

'The interworlds are worlds that are hidden between the realms that most of us can see,' he explained.

Mia looked confused, so he went back further.

*'According to legend, about two hundred years ago, Morgana travelled across the Great Lake, to an in-between world called The Wastelands. She tried to take the throne from the queen, but the queen was more powerful than Morgana, and she defeated her. Then she banished Morgana to the far side of the lake, and placed her under an enchantment, so that she could no longer see, or harm, the outside world.'*

Job heard Mia shuffling and realised that he had rudely left her standing up. He paused to unhook his cloak from a branch, and laid it on the ground, gesturing for her to sit down. Then he continued.

*'Three years ago, while Merlin was sailing across the lake on a tall black ship, he discovered Morgana's home. She bewitched him, and he broke her enchantment and brought her back to Camelot.*

*She was introduced to everyone at court, including King Arthur, and we all loved her, but none of us knew that she was an ancient witch in disguise, or that she was biding her time, planning to take the throne for herself. She fooled us all for a long time, until some of us began to grow suspicious. Merlin secretly used his magic to protect Camelot from her dark spells, but she found out and put him under a spell that weakened him, and he wandered off, no longer able to save us. No one heard from him again.*

*With Merlin out of the way there was no one to stop her, and she waged war against King Arthur. He called upon kings and queens from other worlds to help him, and they brought their armies, but it was no use. She cursed them all. From the roof, I watched as the king, and everyone I knew… knights, dragons, good witches and wizards… were defeated and turned to stone.'*

Job lowered his head, and Mia felt sorry as she saw the sorrow wash over his face. An unexpected splash of cold water hit her on the neck and made her jump. She turned to see her cloud companion raining sad tears over Merlin's letter again. She moved it away from her and the cloud followed.

'What happened next?' she asked, sitting back down.

'She put them all in the tiled hall and turned it into a barbaric museum for herself. I don't have to tell you, you've seen it, haven't you!'

Mia nodded.

'The whole of the royal household is in that dungeon. Well, one day I saw her bringing in Merlin. She had obviously found him out in the wilderness and cursed him too. She had forbidden me to go down there but I would go most days anyway. I miss them, you see, and I know that they can hear me… beneath the spell. I want them to know that they have not been forgotten. Well, some months ago Morgana caught me down there, talking to them, and threw me out of the castle. I have lived out here in the forest ever since.'

'Why didn't she turn you to stone too?' asked Mia.

'Well, she must have been in a good mood that day,' he said. 'Either that, or she has plans for me,' he added, gravely.

Job's sad eyes looked at Mia, then he turned his head towards the dripping red leaves above. 'Y-you see,' he said, struggling to get his words out. 'I-if I can't keep the inside of the castle looking beautiful any more… then I can at least keep the outside looking smart for them, you know?... until they come back. Otherwise… w-what else will I do with my time?'

They shared a silent moment, as they both realised the madness of what he was doing. Mia smiled kindly, then stood up and got ready to leave.

'A-anyway,' said Job, brushing himself down and forcing himself to sound more positive, 'I can't sit around here talking all day. I've got work to do!'

He got to his feet and began to hopscotch jovially back up the ladder. When he was halfway up, he turned to wave goodbye to Mia, but then he suddenly stopped and pointed into the trees.

'Watch out!' he yelled. 'Behind you!'

5

# SIR MORIEN

*In Camelot there are magical things.*
*Some have long horns, and others have wings.*


Mia turned around and saw a bright light moving through the trees.

'It's the white stag,' called out Job. 'He travels through the interworlds, moving among people that we cannot see.'

The huge stag came into view and stopped to look at Mia. Its long antlers glowed against the dark ancient trees, and gave off a sparkling, hypnotic aura that made her begin to feel sleepy.

'Ooh, bad luck,' she heard Job hiss in her ear, as she was drawn unwillingly towards it. 'He's got you now.'

Her arm lifted and reached out to the stag, but it bolted.

'Follow him,' Job's voice rang through the air, and in a dream-like state Mia gave chase, until the world of the strange man was far behind her. For miles she ran, leaping without effort over fallen trees, and charging through rocky streams, never once losing sight of the glowing, magical creature as it raced through the forest, kicking leaves and twigs into the air with its back feet, and transfiguring them into enchanted creatures, which darted around her feet. At no point did Mia feel like stopping, and for the first time, she felt the thrill of being in Camelot.

Some time later, the stag came to a halt, and the hypnotic feeling immediately ended, leaving Mia exhausted. She slumped to the ground as the stag gave her one last glance over its shoulder, and then bounded away into the trees. While rummaging around in her bag for some water, she realised that the gloomy cloud was missing. Worried that she had lost her only friend in this insane place, she was relieved to see it zigzag through the trees a moment later and crash land on her bag. It amused her as it lay there, panting, and she poured some water over it to perk it up.

They were in an apple orchard, and the subdued light was beginning to break through the clouds, making the fruit look fresh and inviting. Mia picked the greenest one she could find and ate it as she strolled on. It was not long before she noticed a young man sitting in a muddy patch beneath one of the trees.

His knees were bent, with his arms and chin resting on them. He looked miserable, hunched up with his own miniature raincloud hanging above his head and pouring down on him. Mia instantly recognised him as the knight from the picture in Stickney's bookcase.

'Sir Morien!' she shouted, running over to him in an over familiar way that she was soon to realise was not very sensible.

The knight was startled and quickly stood up, drawing his sword.

'Who are you?' he demanded.

'Oh, sorry. My name is Mia,' she said, nervously, putting her hands up. 'I- I have something that belongs to you.' With a single finger, she pointed at her backpack.

As soon as the knight saw the gloomy raincloud hovering above it, he lowered his sword and grew excited.

'You have my letter!' he exclaimed, rushing over. 'Is Merlin with you?'

'No… sorry, Sir Morien,' she replied. 'Merlin has been cursed by Morgana. He won't be coming. I've come to help you though, if I can.'

Mia saw his face drop. Mia thought that he looked quite a sorry sight to say that he was one of King Arthur's knights. Realising that the girl was not one of Morgana's spies, he assured Mia that she could lower her arms.

'Call me Morien,' he said, taking the letter.

The moment the knight opened the parchment, the two gloomy clouds joined together, combining to form a single fluffy ball, which floated away and dispersed into a vapour of white silky wisps. Mia held up her hand to say goodbye, feeling sad by the loss of her companion.

'I suspected as much,' Mia heard Morien say, turning her attention back to him. He had removed his cloak and was wringing out the water. She stepped back to avoid the soggy bog that he was creating in the soil.

'I sent that message by enchantment to Merlin some years ago. I wondered why it never reached him.'

'It *did* reach him,' explained Mia. 'It was hovering next to him when I found him. Maybe he read it before he was cursed?'

Morien hung his cloak on the tree to dry.

'When an enchanted letter is sent, it leaves behind a cloud over our heads, until we receive a sign of hope,' he said. 'It would have disappeared if Merlin had read my letter. As it remained with me, I knew that he had not.'

Then he smiled at Mia. 'But it left me as soon as you arrived, so you must be good news for Camelot,' he said. 'Where did you say you found the letter?'

'In the tiled dungeon under the castle, where Morgana has put all of the cursed people,' she explained.

As soon as she mentioned the tiled hall, Morien's eyes lit up.

'How did you get in there?' he asked. 'Morgana sealed it shut with an enchantment.'

When Mia told him about the tunnel in the castle moat, Morien looked very puzzled.

'I know Morgana,' he said. 'She is crazy, but she protects her sorcery well. She would not just leave a doorway to the dungeon open for anyone to find.

'Unless she *wanted* me to find it?' gulped Mia.

'I doubt that is true, my friend,' he said. 'I think that you broke her spell somehow. It has only happened once before, and by someone not of this world. Someone like you!'

Morien laughed and shook her hand with great enthusiasm. 'Welcome, Mia! You may just be the one to save Camelot!'

Mia was quite taken aback that Morien had guessed her secret.

'You said that someone not of this world had broken one of Morgana's spells before?' she queried.

'Yes. When I was a young boy, King Arthur told me of a man named Oliver who once visited Camelot on a flying tree. It was Oliver who had discovered Morgana's dark magic and warned Merlin of her plans.'

Mia was astounded. *Mr Oliver!* she thought. That lovely old man from the playing field was a time-traveller too? She could not believe it. She would certainly have a few more questions for him when she saw him again. *If* she ever saw him again.

'It seemed like just a tale at first,' continued Morien, 'but I have since witnessed many strange things on my quests, and I've visited realms where the veil between two worlds is so thin that creatures travel from one to the other easily. It is no accident that you found us.'

A feeling of dread filled Mia. She knew what was coming next and had already decided that the answer was going to be *no*. Morien smiled at her reassuringly.

'So, Lady Mia,' he said, chirpily, picking two apples from a tree and throwing one to her. 'It seems that you have unwittingly volunteered yourself to take Merlin's place and destroy Morgana's magic. Are you prepared to come on the quest with me to save Camelot?'

Mia chomped into her apple, half regretting having picked up Morien's book that morning. A deafening clack of thunder rang out. She looked to the sky and saw dark stormy clouds moving in at great speed.

'Looks like rain,' she said.

Morien shook his head slowly. 'Those are not rainclouds.' He reached for his sword. 'Morgana's magic is shifting. She knows you are here and is searching for you.'

A high-pitched scream made them duck for cover, then the hundred black crows that had chased her at the castle tumbled out of the clouds and hurtled towards them.

'Quick! Hide me!' she begged, taking flight.

Morien grabbed her arm and they dived into the safety of the undergrowth. There they hid in silence until the storm clouds moved away, taking the birds with them.

'I can't go with you now!' cried Mia, pulling the twigs from her hair. 'She's looking for me!'

'Do not underestimate your power over that witch,' said Morien. 'You have already broken through one of her spells, unharmed. Please. You are our only hope of destroying her.'

As much as Mia wanted to believe it, she doubted that it was true, but Morien's face was so full of hope that she agreed once more to help him.

Morien's small stone house was just beyond the orchard. When he opened the door, Mia could smell something cooking, which made her feel hungry.

'Here! You will need this,' he said, throwing her a thick woollen cloak. He then pulled a short sword from the cupboard and tested its sharpness on the stone fireplace.

'This will be good enough for now,' he said, handing it to Mia, and taking another sword for himself. 'But we will need weapons far more powerful than these if we are to protect ourselves from what lies ahead. We will find what we need in the dragon realm.'

'The dragon realm?' said Mia with wide eyes.

There was no response from the knight. He was carefully removing the pot of stew from the fire and spooning it into two bowls.

'Eat up,' he said, sliding one along the table towards Mia. 'We have a long and dangerous journey ahead of us.'

# 6

# THE PERILOUS JOURNEY

*When there's no turning back, you must forge on ahead.*
*But if you take the wrong turn, you may end up dead.*

Their quest led them East, and towards the dark mountains. The forest surrounding Morien's house was wild and overgrown, which gave Mia the opportunity to practice using her new sword before they reached a clearer track. She was struck by the number of abandoned watermills they passed along their route, with their once industrious wooden paddles standing idle and rotting away in the slimy polluted water.

'What happened to everyone?' she asked, peering through the window of a deserted building.

'They were no longer needed,' answered Morien. 'These millers would have supplied bread and flour for Camelot but now of course...'

'It looks like they left in a hurry,' she said, noticing the toppled over furniture and discarded pots. 'I hope they escaped safely?'

'If they were *lucky*!' said Morien, crouching down to scrape the blanket of dark weed from the paddles with a stick. He fished more of it from the river, screwing up his face at its putrid smell.

'This has choked the river and stopped it flowing,' he scowled. 'We used to fish here, but any living creature has long since departed.'

When he got no response, he turned around, just in time to see Mia slumping forwards, about to fall headfirst into the water. Morien grabbed her collar and pulled her back. She was in a trance. When he investigated, he saw black shadows dancing beneath the surface, twisting and turning, beginning to hypnotise him. He hurled a stone into the swirls, driving the apparitions away on a series of ripples, and releasing them both from the spell. Mia woke up and shook the dazed feeling from her head.

'What happened? I feel strange.'

'Stay away from the edge,' warned Morien. 'Those shadows were conjured by Morgana. They were the toxic waste from her spells. She pours what is left in her cauldron out of the castle window, and then the goo crawls towards the river, killing everything in its path.'

'What spell do you think that was?' cringed Mia.

'I don't know,' replied Morien, 'but you can be sure that it ruined someone's day. Come, let's get far away from here.'

They hurried on as fast as they could. The trail took them deep into the forest, where the trees were ancient and gnarled. Scattered among them were the grey fossilized trunks of former trees, sticking out from the ground like tombstones.

'This is the oldest part of Camelot,' explained Morien. 'There are creatures here that even I have never seen. We must stay on our guard.'

He raised his sword in front of him and Mia did the same, as they walked into a tunnel of trees that had intertwined their branches to form an arch. A few steps in, the noise of the forest disappeared. All that Mia could hear was her heart beating, and the sound of blood rushing through her ears. To distract herself from the creepy feeling it gave her, she counted her footsteps until they got to the end, where she was comforted by the sounds of the wind and birds once more.

From then on, their journey became easier, and they passed the time joyfully finding out about each other's lives.

'You can travel seventy miles in one hour?' cried Morien in astonishment… 'and without horses? My goodness! That is even faster than a dragon!'

He was highly entertained by Mia's stories of the modern world, and she was delighted by this. She enjoyed teaching one of King Arthur's knights. It made her feel very intelligent, and with each tale she told him, she became bouncier and more animated. Mia had never felt particularly bright at school. She usually struggled to understand what the teacher was saying, and no-one *ever* told her that she was intelligent. But seeing Morien taking in every word, made her feel *very* intelligent. After that she came to the conclusion that being intelligent just meant that you knew more about a certain thing than the person you were talking to. Mia's mind then wandered off, as it often did – especially during boring subjects at school – and she pondered all sorts of things, whether for instance, a sparrow might be thought more intelligent than a doctor, if the subject was how to survive outdoors during the harshest winter or something!

'What *magic* you have in your world!' said Morien, breaking her thoughts. 'It would take me two days to travel that far on my horse!'

She laughed at the suggestion that modern inventions were magic, but after weighing it up, she supposed that science *could* be another word for magic, after all, in science class she had been taught all about potions, unusual creatures, and invisible forces making everything work.

'Where *is* your horse?' she asked, eventually.

Morien's smile dropped from his face, and he paused before plonking himself down on a fallen tree trunk. He picked up a stone and threw it at a small mossy knoll in the distance. The stone sent a chunk of green moss flying into the air, and he clenched his fist in triumph.

'Charger, my horse, is still somewhere in the castle grounds,' he sighed. 'During the battle, Morgana went up to the roof of the castle and cast a petrifying curse over us all. Charger got me safely away and threw me off before it hit her. She was turned to stone along with the others. She saved me but I had to leave her there. I do not know what happened to her after that.'

Mia could see how heartbroken and guilty he felt, and although she could have happily sat down and joined him, the sound of a distant twig cracking on the floor urged them to carry on walking.

'How much further is the dragon realm?' she asked after an hour. Tiredness was getting the better of her and she was beginning to feel cranky.

'It is far away from here,' he replied, 'but we will use the mountain witch's shortcut.'

'Mountain witch?' she groaned. The sound of this was more than she could bear. 'I'm already being chased by Morgana. I really don't need *two* witches in my life!'

Morien laughed out loud.

'Don't worry. Molly Merle is a nice witch,' he reassured her. 'She's a little… let's say, *different,* but she's quite harmless, and she will help us get to the dragon realm.'

A change of weather signalled that they had reached the edge of the forest and had entered the watery realm. They pulled up the hoods of their cloaks to shield them from the sudden down-pour of rain.

'Up there!' said Morien. 'That's where we are going.'

Mia looked up and saw the bent peaks of a sky-scraping mountain range ahead. It looked like a cluster of grey, crumpled witch's hats, and running down them were bright blue streams of water that were firing out blue sparks.

'Those are the Mystical Mountains,' said Morien. 'Where Molly Merle lives.'

The slope looked steep and dangerous, and not at all promising, but Mia was now far too tired to worry, and so, deciding that getting it over and done with as quickly as possible was probably the best strategy, she faked a smile, nodded at Morien, and strode heroically towards them. A roll of thunder hurried them along until they reached the edge of the wide river that surrounded the slopes. Morien pointed up at a gap in the higher rocks, from which a jet of steamy azure water suddenly shot into the air, pouring down the mountain into the river. This was followed by several further eruptions, each brighter and more sparkly than the last.

'They are Molly's magic wells,' he explained. 'Portals to anywhere we want to go.'

'Portals?' exclaimed Mia.

'You will see,' he said. 'Come! Let's keep going. We have a long climb ahead of us.'

Mia was dismayed to see that the rope bridge across the water had collapsed, and that they had no choice but to wade through the river if they were to make it onto the mountain path.

'Is it safe?' she frowned.

'The water is shallow enough at the moment,' Morien answered. 'But rivers can change very quickly. We must go while we can.'

They took off their shoes and socks and stepped into the freezing water. They started walking across the river, but the easily walkable pebbles soon gave way to large round rocks which were slippery, and almost impossible to stand on. The further into the river they went, the deeper the water got, and by the time they reached the middle, it was up to their waists. Mia could barely feel the bottom anymore. She felt frightened seeing how far they still had to go to get to the other side. Matters worsened when, without warning, a violent wind sprung up from nowhere. It howled around the mountain, driven by an unseen force, and within seconds it had whipped the water into a raging torrent. Mia screamed to Morien and clawed desperately at the air as the current began to drag her under. Down she went, her back crashing onto the rocks below. She felt the water fill her mouth as she was swept down the river.

# 7

# THE MOUNTAIN WITCH

*In the Mystical Mountains there are mystical spells,*
*and the sparkling blue puddles are magical wells.*


Mia felt helpless as the waves spun her round and round, until she no longer knew which way was up. Too exhausted to fight it, she closed her eyes and began to sink.

Suddenly, she felt something nudge her legs. Whatever it was, swam underneath her and began to lift her upwards to the surface of the water. Half conscious, she felt someone pulling her to the shore, and then she hit the sand with a bump. The wind died, and the river became calm. Mia coughed and vomited up the slimy, stinky water that she had swallowed, then she looked up and saw Morien slumped next to her, wet and shivering.

'Th-thank you!' she panted.

'Don't thank me,' he wheezed, nodding towards the river. 'Thank our friend over there. He rescued us both.'

Mia turned and saw a giant water dragon, rolling and surfing through the easing swells. It was studying them with its dark grey eyes as it played, and as soon as Mia saw it, it splashed the water with its long tail, then dipped beneath the surface and slithered away.

'I have never known this river to be that turbulent,' said Morien, shaking. 'This is witchcraft. Morgana has found us.'

A screeching noise above made them look towards the sky. A flock of crows were circling them. There was no mistaking the smoke-like threads pouring from their wings.

'That's her!' panicked Mia, clambering to her feet.

The crows moved together, making the shape of a threatening long black witch's cloak, which, after hovering silently for a few moments, fluttered off into the clouds. The two of them hightailed it to a small cave at the foot of the mountain and rested for a while before beginning the long climb. The first part of the track was flat and easy to walk, but then it started to get steeper and narrower. As they got higher, the ground under their feet became a blanket of loose grit that sent them sliding towards the cliff edge with every step. Mia was scared, cold, and hungry, so when, after all that effort, the path led them to a dead-end, she finally lost her temper.

'What now?' she wailed, slumping against the steep wall of rock that had ended their journey.

She noticed Morien checking out the rock face.

Uh oh! she thought.

'We keep going, of course!' he said, confirming her fears. 'But for now, wait here for me.'

Morien found his first foothold and began climbing. After a few minutes his voice echoed down from the top, and a rope came tumbling towards her.

'Put the looped end around your waist and I'll pull you up,' he shouted.

Mia did as she was told and then took a moment to compose herself.

'Are you ready?'

'Y-yes!' she replied, not feeling the *least* bit ready.

Morien began to pull, and Mia held the rope tightly as her feet lifted off the ground. As she was being elevated, she made the mistake of looking down and saw that she was swinging freely over a terrifying gorge. She gripped a small tree that was sticking out of the rock, and refused to let go, but when Morien threatened to leave her there, she suddenly found the urge to continue on.

'Good job!' he joked, when she reached the ledge. 'I'll make a warrior of you yet!'

With the worst part over, Mia felt much happier, and soon they were back on a wider path to the top. The upper part of the Mystical Mountains was breath-taking. They glistened blue, as though they were made from millions of tiny sapphires. The higher Mia and Morien climbed, the more intense the colour became. The path twisted and turned, taking them through a series of bright blue waterfalls, which cascaded down the mountains, and produced blue sparks whenever they hit a jutting rock.

'Here!' said Morien, calling Mia back, and squeezing himself through a hidden recess. 'We have to go through here.'

Mia followed him through the hole, and stepped out into a magical blue forest, where the trees had leaves that flickered like candle flames. The frosty white light brought back memories for Mia, of winter evenings spent walking with her mum. But that was a long time ago, and the thought made her feel sad, so she shook it from her mind. Underneath some of the trees were shallow puddles of water, just as bright blue and sparkly as the waterfalls. Hanging on a chain above each of the pools, was a large bell.

'These pools are magic wells,' explained Morien. 'Portals to take us to other parts of Camelot. When we want to travel somewhere, we stand in the water, ring the bell, and tell it where we want to go. Then, *whoosh*, it transports us there.'

Mia tested the water with her toe.

'Will it take me home?' she asked, reaching out towards the bell. Morien grabbed her hand when it looked like she was going to ring it.

'Using the portals requires great caution, Mia,' he warned. 'They do not possess the power of time travel. If you try, there is no telling where you will end up.'

He saw the longing in her eyes, and in an attempt to cheer her up, he pointed out a discarded pair of cloth shoes that were lying by the well.

'See what can happen if you don't take care?' he said with a serious face. 'This poor fellow must have tripped and fallen into the portal face first. Look, he lost his shoes. Who knows where he ended up! But wherever it was, he will have had cold feet!'

Mia saw Morien's face break into a grin, and they both howled with laughter. It was a welcome release after their emotional day.

'Will this pool take us to the dragon realm?' Mia asked when they had calmed down.

'No,' replied Morien. 'Only one well has the power to transport humans to another realm - the Hydra well - the most powerful portal in the kingdom.'

Morien led them through the forest while he continued.

'The Hydra well opened the gateway between Camelot and the dragon realm but if it is not used correctly, it might transport us somewhere where there is no bell to bring us back.'

The thought of that unsettled Mia.

'That's why we must find Molly Merle. She is the keeper of the Hydra well, and the only one who knows how to use it safely. She will help us on our way.'

A little way down the track, the sound of dull clanging caught their ears. They went over to see what it was. Through the trees Mia could see an old woman in a scruffy purple dress, fidgeting with something in her hand. She was standing in a pool of mud that was covering her feet and hem. Her cone shaped black hat was bent at the end, just like the peaks of the Mystical Mountains, and was pushed to the side as though she had been scratching her head.

'Molly Merle!' boomed Morien loudly, causing the woman to jump out of her skin and drop the object she was holding. She spun her head around, and her face instantly lit up.

'Well, if it isn't Sir Morien!' she exclaimed, with her hand still placed firmly on her chest. 'This *is* a welcome surprise.'

Molly pulled her feet from the mud and squelched over to greet her old friend.

'I haven't seen you for what must be well over a year,' she beamed as they hugged each other warmly. 'What brings you this way?'

Before he could answer, she spotted Mia.

'And who is this?' she enquired, stretching out her arm and shaking Mia's hand, warmly.

As soon as their hands touched, the sky darkened, and storm clouds moved in once more. A terrible gale filled the air, and the witch gripped Mia's hand so tightly that she let out a cry of pain. Molly's eyes turned stony white like the statues in the dungeon, and Mia tried desperately to pull her hand away, but the more she pulled, the tighter Molly's fingers clutched on. Then Molly's voice changed.

'You come from a world that is far beyond that which my portals can reach. When you broke through the barriers of time, you brought with you an energy, greater than any we know. Morgana feels it, and she is hunting the one who has the power to destroy her.'

A loud breathy exhale ended the speech, and Molly released Mia's hand. The air became still once more. The witch, who was visibly shaken, staggered woozily towards Morien, leaving Mia alone, nursing her throbbing fingers.

'You must proceed with caution,' she whispered into his ear. 'Morgana is near.'

Morien took a step forward and helped Molly to steady herself. 'That is why we need your help,' he said, 'to get to the dragon realm. We must get the flame sword if we are to stand any chance against her.'

'And what makes you think that Tarask will just give it up?' she said, patting his hand firmly. 'Knights! You never change, do you? Always stealing from dragons, and then running to me to heal your wounds. Those of you who *make* it out alive that is!'

She walked away tutting and shaking her head, while Mia strode over to join Morien.

'Going to the dragon realm is risky enough,' Molly reminded him, 'but goodness me! Picking a fight with Tarask? Oh, no no no! …that's just plain stupid!'

'What other choice do we have?' he begged.

The woman ignored him and made her way back to the object that she had dropped on the floor.

Morien noticed the muddy puddle by her feet, and the missing bell that was usually hanging above it.

'What happened to the Hydra well?' he asked. 'Where is the water, and the bell?'

Molly looked embarrassed, then slowly uncurled her fingers, revealing the cracked piece of metal in her hand.

'The Hydra bell is broken,' she cried. 'Look! That's the real reason I can't send you to the dragon realm. I was just too ashamed to tell you.'

'What happened?' he balked.

Mia, still somewhat wary of the mountain witch, inched over to see.

'Well, at sunrise today, I had just returned from my rounds, you know, topping up the mountain wells with water, when I saw a ghastly figure standing by the Hydra well.'

Molly swallowed, adding dramatic effect to her tale as she always did, and then handed the bell to Mia.

'Who was it?' asked Morien.

'I don't know,' she replied, fanning herself, 'but it was an evil looking thing, and I didn't like it one bit.'

Molly's story made Mia feel very jittery, and she scanned the trees, nervously.

'I saw it fly over me like a flock of birds,' Molly continued, waving her arm above her head, 'just as I was walking home. At first, I thought that it was the Merle family blackbirds coming to visit me, so, like you do, I ran to get here quicker, but when I arrived, I saw the flock change shape... into something wicked and...well,' Molly's voice was becoming more and more shaky. 'I-it smashed the Hydra bell with an axe. Then the well water disappeared.'

Morien placed his hand on his sword, as if he was expecting company at any moment. Mia threw down the bell and took a deliberate step away from it.

'I suspect that it was Morgana,' said Molly.

'Probably,' Mia quivered. 'She's been trying to kill me all day.'

'And having failed, it looks like she is now trying to stop us getting to the dragon realm,' added Morien.

Molly looked disheartened. 'It looks like she has won then. Without the Hydra bell to summon the magical well water, I can't get you there.'

Mia picked up the bell once more and inspected it.

"I've tried everything to fix it,' said Molly, mournfully. 'But it is no use.'

'I have an idea,' said Mia, and she delved into her backpack and pulled out a large magnifying glass. *Magnifying glasses*, her scout leader had once told her, *were very useful objects to carry with you on adventures, as they can get you out of all sorts of catastrophic situations,* and this was indeed one of those situations.

'It might not work,' she said, 'but it's worth a try.'

The unusual object fascinated Morien and Molly, and they watched with interest as Mia placed the broken bell in the middle of the dried up well and sat back.

'What now?' said Molly.

'Now we wait,' replied Mia.

They did not have to wait long, as moments later the ray of sunshine that Mia needed started to peep through the clouds. She used the magnifying glass lens to reflect the sunbeam onto the bell's cracked surface, and after an hour the metal began to heat up. Soon it was so soft, that when Morien touched it with a stick, it moved.

'It's melting,' cried Mia, shocked that her plan had actually worked.

'Clever girl!' clapped Molly, barely able to contain her excitement.

'Now all we need to do is smear the metal over the crack to seal it,' said Mia.

Molly Merle rolled up her sleeves and stepped forward. 'Step aside! Moving liquid is my area of expertise!'

She swung her wand and said some jumbled words. As she did so, the molten metal moved like water across the bell's surface, and in no time at all the crack was fixed. Mia and Morien cheered victoriously and danced around each other.

'This will cool it down and top up its magic,' beamed Molly, pouring on some blue water from a nearby well. 'It will be even more powerful now.'

She instructed Mia and Morien to stand back as she re-attached the bell to the hydra well, and pulled hard on the chain. It *clanged* so loudly that the vibrations made blue sparkling water gush up from the well and swirl around in the air like a tornado.

'It's working!' shrieked Molly, throwing her arms in the air.

'Thank you! Thank you! Thank you!' she said, hugging Mia.

Mia was about to respond when an alarming shadow passed over them. They looked up to see a blanket of black birds flying over the forest.

'She's back!' panicked Molly, signalling to Mia and Morien to jump into the well.

'Quickly! You must be on your way before she sees you.'

They leapt into the blue pool and Molly frantically began ringing the hydra bell.

'To the realm of the dragons!' she commanded, as the water became a speeding whirlpool.

Mia and Morien were sucked through the ground, and found themselves floating in a curious galaxy filled with stars and glistening mountain peaks. A giant octopus glided past, and Mia realised that they were under water. She started swimming towards Morien but then felt herself being pulled with force through the water once more. The next thing she heard was a deafening, *CLAAANG!* As her feet hit a hard surface. They had left the portal and had arrived at the land of the dragons.

# 8

# THE LAND OF THE DRAGONS

*They knocked on the door of the old dragon's lair,*
*then listened, and shook when a voice roared,*
*'WHO'S THERE!'*

A warm current of air wafted up the hill, bringing with it the foul stench of wet, sweaty socks, and rotting meat.

'Ugh!' wretched Mia, holding her hand over her nose. She looked into the valley. A series of stone buildings and caves stood side by side, forming a small town like any other, except that this one was filled with hundreds of scaly, feathery, toothy dragons of all shapes and sizes. All along the streets, large puffs of black smoke puthered from the chimneys of small workshops. The town itself was cradled inside

the horseshoe shape of the Hydra Mountains, and
where they opened up, lush forests and fields formed
a natural protective barrier against the outside world. It
was the fields that drew Mia's attention more than
anything. Working the land were dozens of bright
green dragons, which appeared to be planting
saplings. They were wearing wide brimmed sun hats
made of straw, and each dragon was either digging a
hole, planting a tree, or watering it.

'Those are green forest dragons,' said Morien,
noticing Mia's engrossed face. 'Tree farmers. All the
ancient forests in Camelot were planted at one time or
another by the green forest dragons. They spend
every day tending to them and keeping them healthy.'

There was a dull *creeeeak-clack* sound as a
wooden waggon - being driven by a rather flabby,
lumbering dragon - rolled into the field. It pulled up
beside the farmers, and they waddled over to unload
the saplings that were piled high on the back.

An engine roar above made Mia and Morien
jump. They looked up and saw a sleek, mottled
dragon jetting over, carrying a suit of armour in its feet.

It hovered above the doorway of the largest cave and dropped the armour with a loud clatter. Then it flew away over the Hydra Mountains.

'Who lives there?' asked Mia.

'Ah!' said Morien, tugging nervously at his collar. 'That is the home of Tarask – the oldest, largest, and most foul tempered dragon in four realms. You will soon meet him, for that is where our quest takes us.' He gulped… 'Into his lair.'

Mia remembered Molly Merle's warning, and her stomach churned.

'Do we seriously have to go in? He'll kill us!'

'If we want the flame sword and armour, we must take that risk,' he answered solemnly. 'Without them, Morgana will destroy us.'

'So, we're going to die anyway,' muttered Mia under her breath.

'Once we have the sword,' said Morien, 'not even Merlin could destroy it.'

As they were talking, the door to Tarask's cave opened, and a gigantic scaly claw dragged the armour inside.

'Er, remind me how Tarask got the flame sword?' said Mia, imagining that he had reduced hundreds of armies to ashes to steal it.

Morien's answer surprised her. 'I believe that he forged them himself, in his dungeons. The flames down there are not of this world, and anything that Tarask makes is truly powerful.'

'How will we get it?' she asked.

'I have an idea. But we must make a stop first.'

Morien led them down into the valley, using the forest path to avoid being seen by the more unfriendly dragons, and when they reached the edge of the town, they pulled up their hoods and walked mostly unnoticed through the streets.

The smell was unbearable, and Mia had to hold her breath most of the way. Despite this, she was very excited to be in the dragon realm. Her books had always said that dragons did not really exist, yet here she was, walking among them. She could hardly believe it. A group of scruffy youngsters came tearing towards them, chasing each other, and nearly tripping Morien up. Mia had to swallow her laughter when he shooed them away, and one of them ran back and stamped on his foot. They walked a little further before turning a corner and pausing at the door of an old blacksmith's forge. Morien pushed open the door, and they were immediately blasted by a scorching wall of heat and choking black smoke. They could not see anything, but the loud noise of thin metal being scraped along stone told them that the blacksmith was in. Morien held the door open until most of the smoke had blown out into the street, then they went inside. The forge was a windowless stone room, lit in one corner by the warm glowing light of a furnace. Where the flames illuminated the wall, they could see the shadow of a figure at work.

'Good day to you, Gobha!' said Morien, coughing the soot from his lungs.

A gruff, slightly irritated voice came from the darkness. 'Oh, what now?' it moaned. 'I can't get this thing finished at all! Wait there, I'll be with you in a minute.'

Mia squinted, and when her eyes adjusted, she saw that it was coming from a tiny little man - probably only as high as her waist. He was wearing brown shabby clothes, covered in dirt. He picked up a pair of tongs, and pulled a red-hot stick of metal from the flames. Mia was surprised to see him carry it across the room with the ease of a feather, despite it being as long as he was, and she then watched as he laid it on the anvil and hammered it into a long flat blade.

'Who is that?' she whispered.

'He is one of the gnome folk,' replied Morien. 'They are master swordsmiths and armourers. There is no one within eight realms, apart from Tarask of course, that can match them in skill. In fact, they were around long before Camelot was built.'

Mia stood mesmerised, watching the gnome bash the sword into shape.

'It takes a great deal of patience to create these weapons,' he added, 'which is strange because patience is not something that the gnome folk are generally known for!'

Eventually, Gobha held up the sword and inspected it in the firelight. When he was satisfied that it was perfect, he put it down, and directed his two beady eyes towards the visitors.

'Humans!' he blurted, uncomfortably. It was clear that their presence unsettled him. He picked up a round flat glass contraption and stared at them through it. 'The last human to come here without armour was charcoaled by a battle dragon.' He grinned at the thought. 'So, what brings you here?'

He walked around Mia, circling her, and tugging at the bottom of her t-shirt. He started to sniff her clothes, which was the last straw.

'Do you mind?' she snapped, snatching the fabric from his hands.

The gnome's small pokey eyes grew large.

'I didn't mean to offend you, *my dear*,' he sneered, dropping his head to the floor in an over exaggerated bow. 'We don't get many humans around here, especially ones dressed like you. I was just making sure that you weren't a witch.'

'A witch?' replied Mia, sharply. Gobha's bad manners were really starting to get on her nerves. She wiped away the soot that he had deposited on her Jeans. 'Do I *look* like a witch?'

Gobha stayed silent and gave a toothy grin.

'Well, it's hard to tell these days!' he replied. Morien tried not to smirk at Mia's outraged face.

'Anyway!' she continued, huffily. 'How can you tell by *sniffing* someone that they're a witch?'

Gobha glared at her. 'Goodness me,' he snorted. 'Doesn't this girl know anything? Because witches smell of sweet ginger, of course,' he said. 'It hides their foul stench, and they use its scent to carry evil into the nostrils and souls of the weak minded.' He waved in Morien's general direction. 'Like him!'

Morien blushed with embarrassment at the insult.

'Then they trick them into doing things that they would not usually do,' Gobha continued.

'I *am* of sound mind!' protested Morien, wanting to give the gnome a telling off, but knowing that he had to keep him on side – for now at least.

Gobha looked at Morien suspiciously. 'Nothing but witchcraft would have made you foolish enough to enter the realm of the dragons,' he said. 'But then, humans have *always* been stupid. What do you want of us?'

'We are here because we need the flame sword and protective armour from Tarask,' explained Morien. 'But we need to borrow strong shields and swords from you, to protect us when we approach him. Will you help us?'

Gobha raised an eyebrow.

'You mean to *steal* his armour.' He dismissed them with one hand. 'I will not help you with that.'

'No! To *borrow* it!' begged Mia. 'Morgana has taken Camelot and turned everyone to stone. We are looking for a way to break the spell, but we cannot go into the castle without the weapons to protect ourselves.

'What care I of the human world and its problems?' Gobha scoffed. 'I have problems of my own.'

He turned his back on them and once again began examining his newly forged sword. 'He will set you alight, and I will lose some fine weapons when he does.'

'Will you really force us to go and see Tarask unarmed?' pleaded Morien, hating the fact that he was completely at the gnome's mercy.

Gobha slammed the sword onto the table.

'Tarask cares even less. As a child he saw the humans destroy his family and friends for sport, and so-called *honour*. The dragon realm was almost destroyed by the greed of man, and so you should pray that you never have to witness what he will do to protect it from your kind. He will not help you, humans.'

Mia had heard enough. 'Morgana may be satisfied with Camelot for now,' she said, 'but how long will it be before she is bored, and her need for excitement brings her here? She has already found the portal. Some of the dragons might survive her magic, but what about the gnomes? Are your kind strong enough to fight her?'

She saw Morien clamp his teeth together, and she wondered whether she had gone too far. Gobha's face twitched slightly at her words, and the two of them stood in silence as they waited to see what he would do. Then, he finally spoke, more quietly and softly than before.

'There isn't a sword or armour that can protect you from Tarask,' said Gobha. His instinct for vengeance against humans is too strong.'

Mia tried hard to think of something kinder, and more persuasive to say. Then it came to her.

'It's not just humans,' she said. 'There are gnomes and dragons imprisoned in Morgana's dungeon as well. They were cursed in the battle and turned into statues. Hundreds of them. I have seen them, and I'm sure that they are alive and trapped inside their stone shells. Surely, you want to help free them?'

Gobha swivelled round on his heel and looked at her in shock. A tear ran down his cheek. 'My father… I thought that he had been killed in the battle,' he said. 'If there's a chance that he is still alive…' He wiped away the tear and quickly grabbed a large shield and helmet from the wall. 'Tarask knows nothing of this,' he shouted, running from the workshop. 'I must tell him immediately.'

Mia and Morien followed Gobha out onto the street, and watched from behind a large tree as he snuck into Tarask's lair. Hardly a minute had passed before an earth-shattering roar came from within. A fireball crashed through the cave door, smashing it off its hinges and sending it catapulting through the air.

Gobha came flying out with it, smothering his flaming hair and clothes with his hands.

'Get down!' he yelled, as he hit the ground.

Dragons, gnomes, and humans alike, stopped what they were doing and threw themselves to the floor as the monstrous Tarask crashed through the roof of the cave and took to the sky. He beat his colossal brown wings and vanished over the Hydra Mountains.

'Well, he did *not* take that news well,' said Gobha, shaking the soot from his head. 'But now that he has gone, I can take you to the flame sword.'

By candlelight, he led Mia and Morien into Tarask's lair. They walked through piles of human skeletons, which were lying on the floor where they had fallen. All were encased in the armour that had been melted by the dragon's fire, and some were still clutching the handle of the sword that had failed to save them. Stepping around the bones, they continued on through a network of dark caverns, until they came to a closed metal gate. Gobha produced a key from his pocket and unlocked it.

'Stay close,' he warned as they began their journey underground. The air in the lower dungeons felt thicker, hotter, and more exhausting to walk through, as though someone had placed a heavy damp cloak on their backs. A few meters down, Mia began to feel strange, and was struggling to catch her breath. Morien suggested that they rest.

'H-how much further?' she gasped.

'I know why you feel breathless,' teased Gobha. 'You can feel the souls who dwell down here, can't you?'

'Gobha, stop scaring the girl,' ordered Morien. 'There are no other souls down here, except for our own.'

He looked over at Mia and was disturbed to see her nodding at Gobha.

'I-is it haunted?' she asked, dreading hearing the answer.

Gobha laughed. 'They are the twilight travellers - souls who leave their sleeping bodies to visit other worlds.'

Mia looked over at Morien for reassurance, but he was just as spooked as she was, and had already made a mental note of the way out.

'The twilight travellers are well known to the gnome folk,' continued Gobha. 'Some are from nearby realms, but others have passed through the veil from other worlds. They are usually harmless…' He moved closer to Mia and whispered out of the side of his mouth, 'but these travellers are very upset, and not so friendly. They are trapped. They came to look at Tarask but they got lost down here and could not return to their bodies. They have roamed the caverns for years, trying to find their way home.'

'Can't you help get them out?' cried Mia, pressing her back safely against the cave wall.

But Gobha had no time to respond before the air suddenly became ice cold.

'What's this?' he shivered, seeing his breath in front of him. 'This is most unusual for a cave.' Then a short blast of air extinguished the candle, plunging them into darkness. Mia screamed, and from somewhere in the lair a chorus of chilling voices joined hers. She felt icy fingers touch her face and pull her spirit from her body, leading it upwards through the rock, and into a large upper chamber where the ghostly white stag was waiting for her.

In a dream-like state, she climbed onto its back and gripped its antlers. The unearthly creature then took to the air, flying from one world to the next, stopping to watch over the slumbering bodies of the twilight travellers who were still lying where they had fallen asleep. Time had stopped for them. Mia was moved to see an elderly man sleeping peacefully in his armchair, while his dog sat with its chin on his lap, waiting for him to wake up. They journeyed on through another solar system, one that looked nothing like Mia's, and saw a young couple dozing happily under a tree on a beautiful sunny day.

Travelling back, they peeked inside a spacecraft that was speeding through the stars. On board was a small child, sleeping soundly while her mother cooked food on a circular red flame. The stag bounced forward once more and they entered a cold dark tunnel. A moment later they were in the tiled hall, suspended above the cursed statues. For the first time, Mia could hear the tortured souls crying for help. She clutched her ears and begged for them to stop as the ghostly face of each man, woman and creature, walked towards her.

Suddenly, she felt herself being shaken by Morien. She opened her eyes, unsure whether she was awake or asleep. After drifting in and out of consciousness, she eventually came round and saw that she was lying on the floor of Tarask's lair. Gobha was holding the re-lit candle over her.

'I'm getting out of here!' she cried, stumbling to her feet.

A wide smile spread across Gobha's face. 'Before you have what you came for?' He pointed to a nearby door. It took the strength of all three of them to push it open, but when they did, they found ten suits of armour, glowing in a magical orange light. Hanging on the wall, and glowing even more brilliantly, was the flame sword.

'Look!' laughed Morien, walking around the room to take it all in. 'We have found it.'

'Incredible!' gasped Mia.

'Yes,' said Gobha. 'The radiance is only given by weapons that are made from dragon fire. My ancestors made them down here in this workshop, in Tarask's flames. The gnomes have worked side by side with the dragons for centuries, which is why they let us live among them.'

Mia picked up a smaller sword that was lying on the table.

'That sword has power enough to protect the bearer from ancient magic,' Gobha said proudly. But it is the flame sword that you will need to survive Morgana.'

Morien had already taken it down from the wall and was swinging it in front of him, gripping its black dragon tail hilt with both hands. 'The most powerful sword in all the realms,' he said, in awe of its lightness. 'King Arthur always told me that this weaponry existed, but I never dared to believe that I would get to hold it.'

'You *must* have believed,' said Gobha. 'Otherwise, it would not have brought you to it. Only those who have true faith can find what seems impossible.'

Armed with the flame sword, and wearing dragon armour, Gobha, Mia, and Morien made their way out of Tarask's lair.

Mia rubbed her eyes, thankful to see daylight again. They turned to thank Gobha but saw that his eyes were fixated on the sky. He made a strange whistling noise, and a moment later a young mountain dragon flew into sight, and skidded to a halt next to them.

'He will take you back to Camelot,' said Gobha. 'I will meet you there.'

Mia and Morien climbed on the back of the beast, and soon, the land of the dragons was far below them.

9

# THE CASTLE GUARD CATS

*With their tough metal helmets and long shiny spears,
they have guarded the castle for thousands of years.*


They had not been in the air for long when another grim shape appeared in the sky in front of them. A tube of green cloud was rotating around an enormous black hole and the dragon seemed to be heading straight towards it. Mia and Morien cried out for the dragon to stop but it took no notice, and soon the gaping dark pit started to drag them in. There was nothing they could do but hold on tight as the black hole spun them around, until they were so disorientated that they had no idea which way was up, or down.

Once more, Mia found herself clinging onto the hope of seeing daylight again, *and* trying not to throw up. Suddenly the hole spat them out, and they felt themselves being catapulted across the sky. Mia opened one eye and saw that they were soaring over the Mystical Mountains. The dragon straightened up and glided over Camelot's villages and meadows before finally dropping them off in the castle forest.

'It knows not to get too close,' said Morien, waving the dragon goodbye.

They made the short walk through the trees and were surprised to find that the castle was still sitting serenely on the hill.

'Where is Tarask?' asked Mia. 'I thought that he would be tearing the walls down by now.'

'Yes!' said Morien. 'It is very strange, and not like Tarask to let this go. But come, Lady Mia, let us not waste time, show me where the portal to the underground hall is.'

He pulled the flame sword from its scabbard and held it up to the sun. The long wide blade gleamed a blood red colour in the light.

'I can use this to break the locks inside the castle,' he said.

As he said these words, the dragon tail handle came to life and tightly gripped his hand.

'This sword is our ally,' he said. 'No barrier will be strong enough to stop us reaching Morgana.'

'Stop turning it!' said Mia, noticing that it was reflecting the sun. We'll be seen.'

Morien, realising his mistake, put the sword away but it was too late. The flashing blade had attracted the attention of a tall dark figure who was standing at one of the upstairs windows.

They ran across the lawn and climbed down into the moat, but the tunnel had gone, replaced by a mound of undisturbed earth and grass. Mia dug at the soil with her hands but found nothing. She ran around the moat in confusion.

'It was definitely here,' she said.

'Morgana has obviously moved the portal to a new place,' said Morien. 'She will make sure that we do not stumble across it so easily again. Now we must take our chances through the castle gate.'

Mia shivered nervously. 'What if she knows we're here?'

'She undoubtedly *does*!' he answered, looking up at the flock of crows that had appeared out of nowhere. 'That is her watching us now.'

'Why doesn't she show herself properly?' Mia asked, trying to control her trembling chin.

'Don't be too keen to see her,' he warned. 'She is more dangerous than you realise. She knows that you have broken one of her enchantments and is probably watching to see what other powers you have. Give thanks for the peace, for the witch will show herself soon enough.'

Mia's thoughts turned to home, and Stickney. She longed to see him.

'Follow me,' she said when she saw the crows flying away. 'Maybe my magical oak tree can help us.'

They ran across the lawn and into the forest where Mia had last seen Stickney. They found the old oak tree, awake and preening himself.

'Troublesome crawly critters,' he muttered, as he tugged at the spiny ivy that had taken hold of his bark.

'Ah, hello Mia,' he smiled as she helped him to pull off a long leafy strip. 'Are you ready to go home?'

How she wished that she could have said yes, climbed inside his trunk, and left Camelot behind. She looked over at Morien, and he reluctantly nodded, as if to say, 'Go with my blessing if you want to.' But the look of dread that he was carrying deep down, seeped out of his eyes. Mia could not leave him without a friend. She patted Stickney and said, 'We will go soon. I just have something to do first. What do you know about fighting witches?'

Morien exhaled with relief.

'Witches?' replied Stickney. 'I find that they are best avoided. Although, I've been told that they're not all bad once you get to know them!'

'This one is!' cried Mia. 'She's trying to kill us.'

'Oh!' exclaimed Stickney, becoming all flustered again. 'You're talking about Morgana! Well, I cannot interfere in the happenings of the places I travel to, and nor should you. It would not be right. Come, Mia. Let me take you home.' Stickney looked worried.

'Sorry Stickney,' she sighed. 'Morgana started it. I'm just helping to restore things to how they should be.'

Stickney shook his head and carried on picking at the ivy.

'Right, shall we do this?' Mia grinned, giving Morien a high five.

The knight laughed. 'Indeed, my lady.'

They used the cover of the trees to make their way to the side of the castle, and then, keeping close to the stone walls they crept round to the front. Hiding at the bottom of the stairs, they watched the gatehouse. The portcullis was now raised, and either side of it stood two guards. Cats! A black and white one, and a marmalade one.

Each was nearly as tall as a human. And each was wearing a protective breastplate and helmet, with a panel down the middle to protect their noses. On the top, two triangular points were perfectly shaped to fit over their long ears. The guard cats sat with their backs to the wall of the castle, holding a spear in their paw. Mia was stunned. Their eyes were huge round discs of light that shone like beacons. She could see that Morien recognised them straight away.

'They are called Jack, and Jiminy,' he said. 'The black and white one is Jack, and the ginger one is Jiminy. They are brothers. I have known them since I was a child.'

They were not like any cats that Mia had ever seen. 'They look magical,' she said, trying to take in the strange sight.

'Jack is King Arthur's particular favourite,' Morien beamed, not really listening to Mia.

As cats do, Jack sat casually licking his toes as he guarded the gate. He was so absorbed with the salty taste of his foot that he had failed to notice that Jiminy was glaring at him, thrashing his tail from side to side. Morien had seen that look before. Whenever Jiminy was in a bad mood, the mere sight of Jack would send him into a rage. And Jiminy was in a bad mood *now*. Within an instant he had thrown down his spear, pounced on his brother, and another fur-flying scrap had begun.

'Ah, here we go again,' said Morien, laughing out loud at the entertainment.

'Won't they hurt each other?' cried Mia, alarmed.

'You needn't worry about them,' said Morien. 'They are experts in martial arts, and enjoy a little tooth and claw combat every now and again.'

'They have a lot of energy!' she remarked, as the yowling ball of fur tumbled down the castle steps. Despite the fact that it was flying all over the place, Mia observed that their fur was in very good condition for such ancient cats.

'Yes,' replied Morien, 'They never physically age, even though they have both guarded the kings and queens of this realm for thousands of years.'

Thousands of years? Thought Mia. The oldest cat that she knew was her auntie's cat, Elphie, who was twelve.

'And all of the monarchs who ruled over Camelot during that time…' continued Morien '… taught them many different languages. They are clever cats indeed.'

Mia's mind turned back to the *so-called* monarch who was ruling now. She imagined the witch sitting alone in the castle, staring at her beautiful but empty rooms. Mia was no stranger to staring at blank walls in empty rooms herself, and could not help feeling a little sorry for Morgana, and that her life had come to this. The more Mia thought about her, the more intrigued she became, and part of her was morbidly interested in seeing her in the flesh. Morien was still standing with his arms folded, enjoying the friendly tussle when Mia suggested that they sneak through the gate while the cats were distracted.

He shook his head. 'It is not wise to upset them,' he warned. 'The cats fiercely guard whoever is on the throne, without question. They now serve Morgana so we must be careful, or it will end badly for us.'

When it looked as though the fight was never going to end, Morien decided to interrupt.

'Hello, friends!' he yelled.

The cats immediately looked up, still clinging to each other, but now still. They parted and walked back to their posts, smoothing down their fur as they went. Back at their stations, they straightened their crooked helmets, picked up their spears, and sat to attention once more. Morien looked at Jiminy and greeted him with a single deliberate blink, and Jiminy blinked back. Knowing that a cat's attention span is usually quite short, he quickly pleaded his case.

'Old friends!' he began, 'I beg of you to let us enter the castle. We must try and restore Camelot to the happy place that it once was.'

The cats ignored him and looked away.

'We *are* old friends, are we *not*?' he stated, much more firmly this time. 'The guard cats and the knights have always had a mutual respect, and have fought side by side for what is right. Morgana is a false queen. Help us to put king Arthur back on the throne.'

There was still nothing from the cats, and when Mia became frustrated and marched towards the entrance, Jack and Jiminy crossed their spears to block her. Morien took a moment to think.

'Do you remember how my friend Sir Lancelot would bring you fresh salmon from the river?' he smiled, raising an eyebrow. The cats gave Morien their full attention. 'He will bring you more if you help us set him free.'

Then, something unexpected happened. Jiminy began to fade away on the spot. And then completely vanished.

'Where did he go?' asked Mia, spinning around on her heel.

She suddenly felt a light swipe on the ear. Turning her head, she saw that Jiminy was sitting behind her.

'How did you get there?' she puzzled, before he winked an eye and vanished again. This game went on for a good few minutes. Each time Mia whizzed around looking for him, he disappeared and popped up somewhere else. When Jack joined in the fun, Mia soon began to feel a little annoyed and very dizzy.

'Oh, keep still!' she yelled.

'They are playing with you,' Morien laughed. 'They must like you.'

After a while, the cats darted off, flashing in and out of sight as they chased each other through time portals. Mia and Morien decided that now was a good time to run towards the gate, but as soon as they stepped beneath the stone archway the guard cats popped up and blocked their entrance again.

'They're never going to let us in,' sighed Morien, watching Jack turn a large wheel to lower the portcullis.

They were about to walk down the hill to come up with another plan, when they heard hissing and spitting behind them. They turned to see the interlocked ball of fur bouncing down the stairs, once more.

'Don't they ever stop brawling?' sighed Mia. Then she spotted a large square object, lying on the floor where the cats had been sitting.

'Look!' she said, nudging Morien. 'A book.'

Morien looked over to where she was pointing but could see nothing. The cats had disappeared down the hill, so Mia dashed over and grabbed it.

'Go, go go!' she shouted.

They fled as fast as they could and did not stop running until they reached Morien's house. Inside, Mia dropped the heavy book on the table, and it suddenly showed itself to Morien.

'What on earth!' he exclaimed, running his fingers over the timeworn cover. On closer inspection they saw that it was an old journal. The pages inside were crumpled and discoloured, and written on them in a dark stain was an unusual text, laid out in lines like a poem.

'What is it?' asked Mia.

'It's an ancient language, not used in these parts anymore,' said Morien. It is traditionally used for enchantments, which is what *these* are!'

Mia stood on her toes and leaned over to get a better look.

'They are Theban words,' he explained, showing her the rows of symbols. 'The language of the first witches and alchemists. We were taught it during our knight training. Each shape has its own meaning, but it is the combination of shapes used that creates each enchantment.'

Morien silently studied the wiggles and dashes, trying to work out what they meant.

'I do not understand all of it,' he said after a while, 'but whoever wrote it is clearly mad.'

Suddenly, he took a sharp intake of breath and stepped back. 'It is Morgana's spell book!' he cried, excitedly. 'Mia, you found it!' He returned to the book. 'Look! She speaks here of cursing Camelot, and of the war between the interworlds.'

'I can't believe it!' cried Mia, and they danced with joy.

'This book showed itself to *you* at the castle, and not me.' said Morien. 'I have even more faith in your power to defeat the witch now.'

'But how do we stop her?' asked Mia. 'She will be so angry with us when she discovers that it's missing.'

Morien continued to search the symbols for clues, while Mia fidgeted impatiently. After some time, his eyes widened. 'This is it!' he said, tapping his fingers on a page. 'Listen!'

*Their hearts will freeze and turn to stone,*
*then all their blood, and every bone*
*will follow it. They will feel it all,*
*while trapped inside the tiled hall.*

'This is the curse that Morgana used on Camelot,' he said.
'Does it say how to break it?' asked Mia, anxiously.
Morien read on quietly, mumbling the words.
'Here!' he said after a few minutes.

*They look for the magic to break my spells,*
*but only a song from the dream faerie bells*
*will free the defeated that bide in the hall,*
*who idle in stone, while their weak kingdoms fall!*

Morien gripped the back of his head as tears of relief poured down his cheeks.

'This is proof that my friends are still alive,' he said. 'Oh, Mia, for too long I have waited for this curse to end, and here at last, hope is restored.'

Mia gave him the biggest hug. 'There's no turning back now,' she grinned. 'But I have one question! What are dream faerie bells? Where do we find them? And what do we do with them?'

'*One* question?' he laughed.

The weather had turned chilly, so before he answered, he knelt down by the fireplace and lit a small fire.

'Dream faeries are the sprites that play inside our heads when we are asleep,' he explained. 'They bring us our dreams.'

Mia's nose crumpled at the thought of sprites, or anything in fact, playing in her brain at night.

'I'm surprised that you don't know about them,' he continued. 'Haven't you ever wondered where your dreams come from?'

Mia looked at him like he was crazy, but then she suddenly remembered that people's beliefs in medieval England was ruled by superstition. Then she began to panic that the dream faerie creatures might be superstition too, and that they might not exist at all!

'I've never seen a dream faerie,' she remarked.

'Not many people have,' said Morien. 'They do not like to be seen.'

'So, how can they break the curse?' she asked, trying to shake off her doubts.

'A dream that a faerie brings us, enters our heads through the music of their bells,' he replied. 'And from what Morgana's spell book says, it seems like we can use those same dreams to send messages to the minds of our cursed friends, and help set them free.'

'But how do we find a dream faerie?' asked Mia.

Morien thought about it for a moment, then said, 'I know *exactly* how!'

## 10

# THE DREAM FAERIE

*There is only one way to get dream faerie bells*
*You must fall fast asleep by the magical wells.*


Within the hour Mia and Morien were making their way back up the Mystical Mountains. They moved more slowly this time as tiredness was beginning to take hold. Mia stopped for a moment to rest, gazing upon the beautiful landscape over which the sun was now setting. The forests below seemed to stretch to the end of the Earth. At home, the only green view she had was the playing field at the back of her house. The rest of the town was mostly houses and shops. She inhaled deeply, filling her nostrils with the fresh, warm air.

Looking at Morien in the distance, Mia suddenly felt very proud of her important part in this adventure.

She had never really felt needed before, or that she fit in anywhere, but now she most definitely *was* needed, and it felt good. She began to imagine all the books that might one day be written about her adventures with Sir Morien. *Mia - the saviour of Camelot*, they would call her, and the thought made her walk with a spring in her step.

'Please tell me about Sir Lancelot,' she said, skipping towards Morien. 'I used to read about him in my adventure books.'

Morien slowed down his pace slightly to allow Mia to catch him up.

'Lancelot is a good friend,' he began. 'When I arrived here from Africa as a child, he greeted me as a brother, and we were never apart after that. We had many adventures growing up, and even did our knight training together.'

Mia immersed herself in his tales until the last of the sun disappeared below the horizon, and they squeezed themselves through the nook that led to the blue forest. Night was falling, and it was bitterly cold, so as soon as they reached the first of Molly Merle's wells, they decided to build a fire and rest. They snacked on cheese and fruit as they warmed themselves, and it was not long after, that Mia's eyelids grew heavy.

'Feeling sleepy?' said Morien.

Mia yawned and nodded.

'Great! Time to put our plan into action.'

She wrapped her cloak tightly around her, curled up next to the well, and went to sleep. Morien hid himself behind a nearby gorse bush and waited for the dream faerie to arrive. He passed the time thinking of what Mia had told him earlier in the day - that dragons and witches did not exist in her world. His heart felt heavy because he knew that this could not really be true, and wondered what had happened to make them hide out of sight. He smiled at the thought of his friend Lancelot being written about as a romantic character in books, and desperately wanted to tease him about it, but then the sharp lonely pain of being unable to, hit him.

A rumble above the blue forest made him look up. The black sky was now lit with flames as Tarask flew over, followed closely by a small army of dragons. They were heading in the direction of the castle.

So it begins, he thought. He looked towards the well. Mia was still sound asleep. 'Come on, dream faerie,' he said under his breath. 'We are running out of time.'

Suddenly, out of the corner of his eye, he saw a flash. He turned his head but there was nothing there. He stood perfectly still. There it was again, only this time brighter, and more powerful. A series of tiny lights suddenly began to explode from the well, popping loudly like bottle corks. Faster and faster the sparks came, magically transforming into bubbles as they hit the air. As they fell, they bounced across the muddy forest floor and surrounded Mia.

Morien watched, wide-eyed as the bubbles then rose, and merged to become one larger transparent ball, which itself was only a few inches high. Inside it, sat a winged creature, creaking back and forth on a rocking chair. Dangling above her head was a short rope, and in front of her was a lever. Morien held his breath and clenched his fists with anticipation.

The dream faerie pushed on the lever and steered the bubble silently down to the ground, parking it next to Mia's head. Morien kept perfectly still, knowing that if the dream faerie saw him, she would disappear. It was, after all, stated clearly in their rule book.

*Rule no.2: A dream faerie must never allow a human to see him or her.*

Once, when he was a child, Morien found a discarded faerie rule book on his pillow, and read it from cover to cover before the forgetful sprite came to collect it the next night. The dream faerie stepped out of the bubble and stood beside Mia's head.
Then she produced a small bell from her pocket and calmly began ringing it. Musical notes appeared on the breeze and formed pictures that floated into Mia's ear.

Morien saw the hazy images of Mia's world pass before him, and the visions frightened him. He recognised nothing.

There were tall thin stone castles crammed side by side, into which countless people ran in and out. He saw Mia running towards Stickney Pygott, but why was he standing alone? Where were all the trees?

Morien could not take his eyes off this strange world. When the last dream had been released into Mia's brain, he stepped out from behind the bush.

The dream faerie jumped back in shock when she saw a human standing in front of her, but Morien knew that it was safe to do so, as she was not allowed to vanish from sight now that Mia was dreaming. He had also remembered *that* from the book.

*Rule no. 6: A dream faerie must <u>never</u> break someone's dream halfway through, as this will trap the person in the dream realm forever, and they will become the eternal responsibility of the rule breaking faerie.*

Knowing that the dream faerie was forced to stick around until Mia's dream was fully played out, the knight took his chance to speak to her.

'Do not be afraid,' he said, reassuringly. 'I am not here to harm you. I need help.'

For a moment it looked as though she was going to flee back to her bubble, but she remained where she was and continued ringing her dream bell over Mia. Her eyes remained firmly fixed on Morien. He began to tell her about the curse of Camelot, and explain how they needed her bell to break Morgana's spell. The dream faerie listened patiently until Morien had finished, and then she silenced her bell, commanding the dreams to leave Mia's head. Mia instantly opened her eyes and was stunned to see the dream faerie looking at her. As she sat up, the faerie grabbed hold of one of the departing dreams and waved her wand around it. The pictures began to change as a curious sound came out of her mouth, a haunting, beautiful melody that blew through the trees. Mia and Morien watched as the swirling dream played them the faerie's answer.

*The grey witch whose hair floats above her like branches,*
*stares at you with eyes that can cause avalanches,*
*and great fires, and plagues, and fierce lightning strikes*
*that will turn you to stone, and then she takes what she likes.*
*A long time ago, the witch travelled this land,*

*swishing her wand and then raising her hand,*

*to turn into statues, great knights, kings and*

*queens,*

*and wizards, and dragons, in great battle scenes.*

*And all of them now stand as statues, enchanted,*

*in a great tiled hall, until my song is chanted.*

*My bell will ring out and fight Morgana's curse*

*but it will not be easy, as she will bring worse.*

*Not all will survive her treacherous spell*

*but we shall start in the place where the petrified*

*dwell.*

The pictures faded as the faerie song ended. She had agreed to help them. And so, with only the moonlight as their guide but much hope in their hearts, the three of them started the long journey back down the Mystical Mountains, and towards Camelot.

# 11

# MORGANA

*A spell that is starting to slowly unstitch,*
*is a terrible thing for a hideous witch.*

The grey witch crawled up the spiral staircase to the highest turret in the castle and stared out of the window. The cloud that was disturbing her was moving more swiftly now, like a meteorite of steam, charging across the black sky. She squinted. Her eyes were not so good these days, but she was certain that it was not being driven by the wind as other clouds were. It was being pulled from the front by an invisible force. And now fiery flares were blasting from it. She shrieked when the bottom of the cloud suddenly turned green, and a gargantuan dragon swooped down. It nose-dived towards the turret, bellowing as one more blast of deadly flames exploded from its mouth. Then, from the same cloud flew another dragon, smaller, but just as deadly looking, and it was followed by another, and then another.

Mia, Morien and the dream faerie watched the dragons fly over from the forest.

'Come on!' Morien shouted, barely able to hear over the noise. 'We must get to the castle before our friends are destroyed.'

Morgana inched back from the window, knowing that if Tarask saw her he would bring the tower crashing down beneath her feet. She had encountered this creature before, in a battle that had left her body broken and twisted. She limped back down the stairway and hobbled along several dark passages until she reached the dungeon. With a swish of her wand, the door to the tiled hall crashed open.

Morgana stood motionless, momentarily paralysed by the feeling that she was being watched by something not of her making. Her bent fingers fumbled about in the darkness, searching for one of the candles that she kept on a shelf behind the door.

She found one and lit it, and then, holding it out in front of her, the witch twitched and squirmed her way around the statues, checking whether anyone, or any*thing* suspicious was hiding in the shadows. She knew deep down that it was just her prisoners, those living a half-life inside their stony shells, who were staring at her, but since she had discovered that the enchantment sealing the tiled room had been broken, she had lost her nerve. Worrying that old age might have weakened her powers, Morgana decided to test them.

She closed her eyes and called to the incantations that surrounded the statues.

'*Gramarye, Gramarye, veni naeniam.*' she chanted.

The first to show itself was a green, curling vapour that rose slowly from the ground in a corkscrew motion.

Next, a purple swirling vortex appeared in the air.

'*Gramarye, Gramarye Veni ad me,*' she continued, as a display of shooting stars appeared from nowhere and looped around the statues.

She opened her eyes, feeling reassured that the curses were all still there, and untouched. With renewed confidence, the witch began to summon her darkest magic from deep below the ground. She paced up and down the hall with her wand held high, invoking snakes of black mist that slithered across the tiled floor, before joining together to form a threatening hooded creature, which rose up and stood beside her.

Morgana's voice became so low that outside the castle the earth began to tremble.

'What's that?' cried Mia, struggling to stay on her feet.

'I don't know!' said Morien, 'and I'm not sure that I want to. Come! We are nearly there.'

Back in the tiled hall, Morgana was waking the statues and calling them to battle. With a single command, the hooded creature touched each of the stone figures, turning them from white to grey as it breathed a dark life into them. Camelot's half-life kings and queens began to move. They lurched forward, scraping the floor with their feet as they staggered awkwardly towards their jailer. Morgana raised her hand and they stopped in front of her. In one synchronised movement they raised their swords in allegiance to her. A second order was chanted, and the knights of the round table reared up on their horses. Their maces, which had been held frozen above them for so many years, now swung freely. With a hollow whinny, the horses trotted over to the monarchs and lined up behind them, almost smashing to pieces the gnome folk who were coming to life in the walkways.

Last to be called were the cursed dragons. They hopped down from their plinths with a cry so piercing that it brought some of the wall crumbling down. They joined the others. Morgana flung her arms up, and the statues began to march out of the tiled hall. She laughed with pride at the ghoulish parade as they clunked and clomped their way to the castle lawn.

When Mia, Morien and the dream faerie finally arrived at the castle, they were met with a ghastly sight. On one side of the lawn, sat Tarask and his dragon army, and facing them was Morgana's army of possessed statues. Mia touched her stomach to reassure herself that she still had the dragon armour on. She felt sorry for what Tarask must have been feeling, seeing his lost family and friends lined up against him, and when she turned to Morien to ask what they should do next, she saw that something was alarming him up on the castle roof. She looked up and saw a woman standing out on the ledge, lit by the full moon, and looking as gnarled and ancient as the trees of the forest. Morien was taken aback by her appearance. Was this the once great, Morgana le Fey? he thought. The empress whose beauty was once so envied by all at Camelot? The wind was blowing her ragged hair upwards, separating it into branches that swayed from side to side as she surveyed the battlefield.

They watched as the witch raised her wand, and with a blood curdling cry, she ordered the statues to attack.

## 12

## THE BATTLE BEGINS

*A witch who fights fiercely to rule earth and sky,*
*does not care a jot that so many will die.*

The statues lumbered clumsily towards Tarask's army, their stiff heavy legs chopping left and right like scissor blades. The swords and axes that they were holding had been magically transformed back to sharp steel, and were just as deadly as they once were.

Horrified, Mia called out to the dream faerie who she felt hovering by her shoulder. 'Quick! You have to go and break the spell before everyone is killed.'

When she got no response, she turned around and was shocked to see the faerie shaking inside her bubble.

'We're too late!' the faerie quivered.

Mia was surprised to hear her speaking like a human.

'W-what do you mean?' cried Morien.

'My music only works on those who are asleep,' she replied. 'Alas! These poor souls are half awake, and under a much more powerful spell than I can break.'

Mia and Morien looked at each other, completely devastated that their last hope was fading. Without further hesitation, Sir Morien, brave knight of Camelot, drew the flame sword from his scabbard and sprinted towards the battlefield, shouting back at Mia, 'Find my horse and bring her to me.'

'Come on, we need to get into the gardens,' said Mia, giving the faerie's bubble an encouraging prod.

The dream faerie was annoyed by the ill-mannered poke, and gave Mia a disapproving look, before pushing on the lever and driving the bubble forward. Mia could see that the castle gate was raised and unguarded, and decided to see whether they could sneak in without the cats appearing. As they were climbing the hill, Mia glanced behind and saw

Morien standing beside Tarask. The statues were closing in on them.

There were so few dragons, compared to Morgana's troops, and she knew that he would need Charger if he were to stand any chance of surviving. Mia and the faerie ran under the portcullis, unchallenged, and made their way into the castle.

Down on the ground the first attack was not going quite as Morgana had planned. Most of the cursed statues were proving easy to outrun, while the stone dragons were too heavy to fly, and so hopped along the ground in a ridiculous manner. Morien began to snigger when Morgana wailed with frustration but stopped as soon as she ordered the knights to attack. The dragons held their positions as the cursed knights drew nearer - some marching, and the rest charging forward on horseback. Morien was mortified to see his dearest friends ready to kill him. He held up the flame sword and prepared himself to fight.

Tarask's voice boomed out. 'Do you think that your mortal weapons are any match for us dragons?' he bellowed, spraying the knights with a jet of flames.

But to his, and Morien's dismay, it did not slow them down. They continued advancing. Morgana mocked their failed attempts with shrieks of laughter. When the dragons saw her up on the roof they gave chase, leaving Morien alone on the ground. The statues circled him, preventing his escape, and the mounted knights moved closer. Their horses reared up beside Morien, almost crushing him as their hooves crashed back down to the earth.  Clumps of the green mould that covered them, broke off, releasing a putrid damp smell that made him heave. He drew upon his knight training to try and stay calm.

'Stand down!' he eventually said, holding the flame sword above his head. 'The Knights of the Round Table fight for King Arthur, *not* the witch!'

To his relief, the stone army came to a halt. In a unified movement, they turned their heads to face him. Morien looked upon their faces and saw his friend, Sir Lancelot astride one of the horses.

'Lancelot!' he cried, pleading to whatever was left of the soul of his friend.

Lancelot gave no response.

'It is me, Morien,' he begged, 'the son of
Anglovale. Do you not remember me?'

Morien was convinced that he saw a flash of recognition appear in Lancelot's stony eyes, but a second later, a swirling black mist surrounded him, and it was gone.

Suddenly, their swords and maces came crashing down on him. Morien blocked them with the flame sword and managed to escape, running as fast as he could, with the knights in close pursuit.

Mia and the dream faerie had found the walled gardens behind the castle. In the moonlight they could see how neglected they were. Dead plants lay rotting in the sludgy soil, while long, straggly weeds wrapped themselves around the feet of the ornamental statues. They looked for Charger but could not see her anywhere. Passing through a brick archway, they entered a second garden, scattered with overgrown bushes that were once neatly cut spirals and cones. The ponds which were once chockful of wild creatures, now lay empty and drained. On the far side there was an old rusty gate with two statues, one standing either side of it. As Mia approached them, she saw two familiar faces.

'The guard cats!' she cried. The poor creatures had been turned to stone. 'It's all my fault!'

'How can it be your fault?' asked the dream faerie.

'I stole Morgana's spell book from them, and now she has punished them,' she replied.

The dream faerie smiled at her. 'But if you had not taken it, I would not be here,' she said.

Mia wondered whether it would have made any difference whether the dream faerie was there or not. After all, she had been no use so far. It must have shown on her face, as the faerie continued. 'I might not be able to free those that Morgana has brought to life, but when it is safe, I *will* release everyone who is asleep. But for now, they are safer here.' This made Mia feel a little guilty for thinking badly of her.

The sound of dragons fighting made them look up.

'We haven't much time,' said the faerie. 'We must keep looking for Morien's horse.'

The area beyond the gate was like a walled jungle. Prickly brambles formed tangled webs everywhere, blocking their way. The faerie pulled on the rope above her head and the bubble drifted upwards like an air balloon, while Mia cut a path through with her sword. The wild growth eventually gave way to more open lawns, and Mia ran through the rest of the gardens with ease.

As the perimeter wall led them back towards the castle, their attention was drawn to a heavy scrubbing noise. It seemed to be coming from behind a bush that was growing under one of the windows. Mia bent down and looked underneath it. A small candle was burning on the ground. Next to it sat a wooden bucket, and next to that were a pair of pointed cloth shoes, standing on tiptoe. Mia immediately recognised the single droopy brown sock that was crumpled around the ankle.

'Job!' she cried, scurrying round to see the old caretaker.

The man jumped, dropping his scrubbing brush on the floor when Mia and the faerie appeared in front of him. He was removing the mould from one of the old statues.

'Oh, thank goodness,' he exclaimed. 'For a minute, I thought you were the witch.'

'What are you doing here?' asked Mia, 'And why are you cleaning at this time of night? Don't you know what's happening out there?'

A terrifying cackle rang through the air, and Job cowered, covering his head.

'It's okay,' said Mia, 'She is still up on the roof.'

Job continued cleaning. 'I-I was so pleased that you came to talk to me in the forest,' he said. 'Because it reminded me that I still had the keys to the dungeon door… and that I had not been taking care of my lords and ladies.'

He rubbed an ingrained piece of dirt with his finger.

'I've been sneaking them out of the tiled hall, one by one, and getting rid of the fungus. It's extremely damp down there, and grabs hold of them so quickly.'

He asked Mia to pass him the candle, then stepped back to inspect his work.

'Poor old Merlin here, had green patches all over him,' he continued. 'It would have made him feel quite itchy.'

Mia's jaw almost dropped to the floor at his words.

'Merlin?' she spluttered.

Her heart raced as the castle caretaker turned the statue around, revealing the unmistakeable carved beard, pointed hat, and robes of Camelot's most powerful wizard.

'He's asleep!' cried the dream faerie. 'I can free him.'

Mia grabbed her hair in disbelief. 'Job! You amazing man!' she laughed. 'I think that you have just saved Camelot!'

The dream faerie wasted no time in ringing her musical bell over Merlin. Mia and Job watched as his stone shell began to shake and crack as the wizard slowly started to wake from his cursed sleep. Mia jumped up and down, unable to contain her excitement. Suddenly, there was a blinding light and a thunderous blast above, as a bolt of lightning hit the castle. They looked up to see part of the roof and wall collapsing down on them.

"Run!' screamed Mia.

She, Job and the faerie bolted from the path of the falling debris but when they looked back, they saw with horror that Merlin had been crushed beneath the rubble.

# 13

## CHARGER

*A friend in need is a friend indeed*
*but a friend who's a steed is useful.*


'Nooooo!' cried Mia, staring in disbelief at the pile of heavy rocks covering Merlin. She ran to the middle of the garden and looked up at the big gaping hole where the castle roof once sat.

'Poor Merlin,' sighed Job. 'There's no way he could have survived that.'

'It's so unfair,' wept Mia, exhausted by the seemingly impossible task of breaking the curse. 'Why can't we get a break? We were so close to saving Merlin and Camelot. And now we're back at the start!'

The dream faerie tried desperately to find a small gap in the stones to squeeze through and see whether she could reach him, but they were too big, and packed too tightly. It was no use.

'We must go and find Charger,' said Mia, finally. 'Job, have you seen any horses around here?'

He had just opened his mouth to answer when a second deafening bang made them cover their ears. Morgana had conjured up a magical bolt of lightning, and it was zigzagging through the sky in pursuit of Tarask and his army. The dragons soared and swooped to avoid it, and the bolt hit the castle, bringing another section of the roof crashing down.

'Stop!' screeched Mia. 'You're going to destroy the whole of Camelot.'

But the lightning continued, and the group on the ground were forced to dive for cover in one of the stone porchways. The dragons retaliated by bombarding the witch with a stream of fireballs. Instead of running away, Morgana swirled on the spot, painting a protective shield around herself. The flaming missiles exploded on impact and showered fiery rain onto the gardens. Mia grabbed hold of Job's arm for comfort, and together they watched helplessly

as the sparks set the walled gardens alight. Tarask
hung in the air for a time, his colossal wings flapping
to keep him suspended, then he opened his jaws wide
and lunged at Morgana. The witch instantly
transfigured into the crows and made her escape over
the Mystical Mountains. The dragons pursued her,
leaving the air above the castle peaceful and silent. All
that could be heard was the occasional crack of
thunder and dragon roar in the distance.

With the danger gone, Job dashed around trying
to put out the fires with his bucket. Mia joined him,
stamping out the smaller ones and covering them with
soil, but despite their attempts, the flames burned on.
Mia was upset about letting Morien down and could
not stop worrying about what had become of him.

Unknown to Mia, Morien was trapped inside a
corridor on the upper floor of the castle. He had
managed to escape the clutches of the cursed statues
by running up the castle hill, knowing that their heavy,
clumsy limbs could not easily follow, but the collapsing
roof had blocked the doorways either side of him,
caging him in. He was clambering over the pile of

rubble, when he heard the *clunk, clunk* sound of the statues approaching.

They were inside the castle, and close. Morien pushed two large stones forward until they tumbled down, landing beneath a part of the wall that had crumbled. Then he climbed on top of them and pulled himself up through the gap.

He looked over the wall and saw that he was at the top of a large fireplace. Warm ashes were still glowing in the grate. He jumped down and stepped out into the state dining room where he had shared many a fine dinner with the king. The outer wall was gone and he could see the flames and smoke rising from the burning gardens below.  Scrambling down the ivy outside, Morien jumped to freedom. He found Mia and Job stamping out the last of the fires, while the dream faerie carried water over on a train of bubbles. Soon, the flames reached the damp leaves on the soil, and began to fizzle out. The caretaker breathed a sigh of relief.

They were all pleased to see Morien, especially Job who greeted his old friend with a hug. Their reunion was interrupted by the *clanking* sound of the statues in the distance.

'Did you find Charger?' Morien asked with urgency. They shook their heads, but Mia told him about Merlin, and how close they were to saving him. Morien looked very sad.

'So that's that then!' he sighed. 'Poor Merlin.'

The *clunking* sound appeared again, only this time it was much closer.

'They are almost upon us,' warned Morien. 'I need my horse if we are to stand any chance against our cursed friends.'

The statues suddenly appeared, marching around the outside of the castle.

They all panicked, and Job fumbled nervously for his keys. He ushered everyone into the next garden, and as soon as they were all safe, he locked the rusty gate behind them.

'We have no time to waste!' said Morien. 'We stand more chance if we split up.'

The group separated, and all headed off in different directions. Mia followed a path that traced a small stream. Halfway down, she passed a cluster of royal statues. Their eyes stared at her. She stopped dead, her heart skipping a beat, until she realised that they were still sleeping, forgotten by Morgana, and rotting away. As she carried on running, the noise of the leaves crunching beneath her feet obscured the faint pleas for help that were coming from their mouths.

Further down the path, the stream split into two. Mia followed the nearest one until she came to a small pond. Someone had placed three of the cursed gnome folk around the edge, like common garden ornaments, and to make it even more humiliating, had placed fishing rods in their hands.

A light breeze brought with it the charcoal smell from the few trees that were still smouldering. Mia continued towards them, until something glistening in the moonlight caught her eye. It was big and bulky, and was poking up through the charred grass. She took out her torch and aimed it at the object. It looked like green marble. Mia began to scrape away the mud and grass, and discovered that it was a horse's head.

'I think I've found her!' she squealed to the others. Morien was the first to dash over. He removed the mud from its back, knowing exactly what he was looking for, and when he saw it - the saddle that he had been gifted upon completing his knight training, he sat back on his heels, and wept. 'Charger!' he whispered. 'Don't worry, my princess. We will soon get you out of here.'

After some digging, and a great deal of excitement, the marble statue was pulled out of the soil. Like the other statues, her body had been frozen in the same position as when the curse had hit her. Her legs were in mid canter, and her mouth was dripping with saliva.

'Thank goodness you are still in one piece!' said Morien, stroking her gently on the nose.

The noise of the garden's metal gate being rattled silenced him.

'Thank goodness it's locked,' quivered Job.

'Stand back!' cried the dream faerie. 'The half-life ones are coming.'

She took out her bell and began to wave it over the marble horse. A stream of musical notes appeared in the air, floating in from every part of the universe.

They danced around Mia's head before settling over Charger and the other sleeping statues. Then the faerie began to sing. It was a strange melody that drifted along with the bell's chimes, until they finally joined each other in a magical harmony. Mia was spellbound, and she was not the only one. A quiet sigh came from each of the statues as the music waltzed around, forming a coil of vibrant colours. The notes touched each statue lightly, bouncing from one figure to the next and making them shudder. Then they moved together, creating a swirling vortex around the horse, causing her shell to vibrate, and forging cracks along her marble prison. Brilliant green light burst from every chink, a second before the statue shattered into tiny pieces, freeing Charger from Morgana's curse. The horse stumbled to her feet, and then whinnied sharply before rearing up, happy to see the sun again.

The cursed statues were smashing through the lock when they heard the sound. They paused to listen, then forced the gate off its hinges and made their way towards the group. The dream faerie continued to ring her bell and sing, releasing musical notes that surrounded and freed the other sleeping statues. One by one, the cursed members of the royal household opened their eyes and drew breath for the first time in years.

Everyone was so entranced by this magical scene, that no one noticed a single musical note wandering off alone. The tiny enchantment had made its way back to the castle and was now zigzagging down through the tiny gaps in the rocks that covered Merlin. A minute later, a bright light shone out through the tiny gaps, and the huge stones began to separate.

Morien was overjoyed to have his horse back. After thanking his friends, he jumped on her back and raced towards the cursed knights, driving them away from Mia and the others.

When the dream faerie had released all the garden statues from Morgana's spell, the musical notes returned to her bell. Mia and Job gathered up all the confused souls and led them to the safety of the castle chapel.

'I will take care of them from here,' said Job, proudly.

Mia and the dream faerie went back outside to see whether anyone had been left behind. When they passed the collapsed part of the castle, they were stunned to see that the mountain of stone crushing Merlin had been moved, and that the bricks were laying scattered around. There was no sign of the broken statue anywhere.

'How did that happen?' asked Mia, feeling bewildered. 'They were far too heavy for anyone to shift. And where is Merlin?'

The dream faerie tapped her slowly on the shoulder, and a deep voice from behind startled her.

'Are you looking for me?'

14

# CURSES AND DRAGONS

*The flame sword chooses the one with the power
to bring forward light in the darkest of hours.*

Mia turned around, and there in front of her stood
Merlin. His carved, rigid robes were now blowing freely
in the wind, and his wooden staff was casting a warm
light over his long ginger beard. She took a step back.

'Merlin!' she gasped. 'H-how did you get out?'

He was about to answer when he noticed the
dream faerie waving at him.

'Ah, Alhena!' he smiled. 'My dear friend. I must
thank you, for it seems that one of your musical spells
set me free.'

The dream faerie whizzed around excitedly in her
bubble. Mia felt ashamed that she had never thought

to ask the faerie her name. The wizard then answered Mia's question.

'Once I was released from the curse,' he said, 'I was able to cast a spell to move the rocks.'

He placed his hand gently on Mia's shoulder.

'You appeared in my dreams in the tiled hall,' he said. 'I knew that you were sent to rescue us. Camelot shall be forever grateful that you answered our call.'

Then he bowed. Mia felt very embarrassed and awkwardly bowed back, not sure whether she was supposed to or not. Merlin straightened himself up with his staff, but he was very weak, and Mia took hold of his arm to help him.

'You have no idea how pleased I am to see you!' she said, sitting him down and showing him Morien's letter, and then going on to explain everything that had happened since. Merlin listened in silence.

'I don't know what to do next,' she admitted once she had finished. 'It's all a mess. Please help us!'

The wizard looked up to the moon and let out a long slow breath.

'My body and mind are still very fragile from Morgana's curse,' he said. 'My magic will not yet be strong enough to overthrow her.' He saw the look of sadness wash over Mia's face, and he smiled reassuringly. 'I am not saying that I will *not* help,' he said. 'After all, it was *I* who brought Morgana here to Camelot.' Merlin's voice became thoughtful. 'I should have taken her back to the Great Lake as soon as she started her mischief… but,' he said more optimistically, 'you have the dragon armour and the flame sword in your possession now, and our army has a strong leader in Sir Morien. Together, we stand a good chance!'

His words made Mia feel a little more cheerful. The wind suddenly, and noticeably, picked up, and brought with it the sharp snapping noise of leathery wings beating. It became louder and louder, until even those hiding inside the castle chapel could hear it. They all rushed outside and watched as a ridge-backed battle dragon, twice the size of Tarask, flew across the moon. They screamed as it turned and headed towards them.

Mia called out a warning to Morien but he was nowhere to be seen. Everyone ran back into the castle. As they fled down the passages to escape, they felt another blow to the roof, and more of it came crashing down around them.

'Go through the gatehouse to the forest!' shouted Merlin, trying to keep some sort of order. But as soon as the fleeing crowd stepped onto the drawbridge, they immediately recoiled. The battle dragon was circling above them with Morgana sitting on its back, steering the poor animal with cruel, sharp jerks on the reins. Some people reversed back into the castle, but Mia and her companions ran for the trees. The dragon blew a choking hot cloud of smoke over Mia, leaving her disorientated and unable to see or breathe. As it cleared, she was panic-stricken to see the witch conjuring a lava dragon out of the departing black smoke. It twisted and turned as thin fiery rivers appeared all over its body, flowing around scaly islands of ash.

'Run!' bellowed Merlin, as the volcanic dragon soared upwards, dripping red fire from its feet and wings.

Mia ran, but as she was still half blind, she tripped over and landed flat on the ground. She heard the sound of hooves tearing towards her and put her arms over her head, fully expecting to be trampled into the ground at any moment, but to her surprise the horse slowed down next to her, and someone grabbed her arm.

'Having fun?' Morien laughed as he pulled her up onto his horse.

Mia was too dumbstruck to answer as they charged towards the forest. They had just made it into the trees when Morgana brought down another bolt of lightning in front of them. It hit a cluster of trees, and they burst into flames. Mia cried out when she saw who was among them.

'Stickney!' she yelled, running over and smothering the flames with her cloak.

Morien and Job rushed over to help too.

'He's my friend,' she sobbed… 'and my only way home!'

Morgana's chilling voice rang out through the branches. The hairs on the back of Mia's neck stood on end.

'You destroyed my magic,' she jeered, tormenting the young girl, 'so *now* I have destroyed *yours*.'

'You evil old hag!' shouted Mia, furious by all that life was throwing at her. 'It is *us* who will destroy *YOU!*'

The witch's howling laughter rang through the forest before fading into the distance. Morien put a comforting hand on Mia's shoulder. The flames moved further up the trees. Mia searched for water but all she could find were a few rain puddles scattered here and there. She collected what she could in her water bottle, and tried her best to douse the flames, while the dream faerie dropped magical, watery bubbles on the leaves. But they made little impact, and the group of trees continued to burn. Losing hope, Mia turned to Merlin and saw that he was holding his staff above his head. He was chanting something. Suddenly, to her surprise, the gloomy cloud appeared, looking very dark and stormy. Mia and Morien were thrilled to see it again. Following it were nine identical little rainclouds. On Merlin's command, each of them hovered above the burning trees, and rained down hard. They did not stop raining until all the fires were put out, at which point, Merlin fell silent, lowered his staff, and collapsed to the floor. The gloomy clouds floated away. Mia rushed over to him.

'It seems that I'm even weaker than I thought,' he said, trying to catch his breath. 'Summoning my clouds drained what little energy I had.'

There was a rustling in the forest, and they saw the uncursed royal household approaching. They had used a secret undercroft to leave the castle unseen, and were carrying food supplies. After being reunited with his old friends, Morien helped Merlin to a seat, and gave him water.

Mia tried to wake Stickney but there was no sign of life. His bark was charcoaled, and his leaves were gone. Mia put her arms around him, feeling so desperately sad and alone. Her eyes welled up with tears. Somewhere in the distance she could hear the faint *clank clank* of the cursed statues drawing nearer, but she no longer cared. She had lost her friend, and the world that she knew.

'Mia,' she heard Morien's voice say, quietly. 'We must be on the move. We will mourn our friends, later.'

He picked up her sword from the ground and handed it to her. The new royal troops looked at their own weapons and saw that they were battered and rusty. Time, damp, and magic had worn away their sharp blades and smooth steel. Their swords were no longer of any use in battle. They were discussing what to do next when Mia suddenly realised that the dream faerie was missing. She went to look for her. Her search took her to the edge of the forest where she saw a stream of musical notes disappearing over the castle, and towards the Mystical Mountains. A few minutes later, after re-joining the group, Mia heard a loud *clang,* and watched as an army of gnomes climbed out of one of the nearby puddles. One by one they emerged, dressed in fine armour, and carrying newly forged swords and shields. The last to hop out was Gobha.

'Ugh! Gnome folk!' said Job. He had always found them very unfriendly and had never trusted them. 'What do they want?'

'I hope we haven't missed anything,' said Gobha, hauling the last of the axes through the hole. 'It's been years since we had a good fight.'

Mia and Morien were delighted and relieved to see the gnome and his friends, and welcomed them with open arms.

'Sorry we're late,' said Gobha. 'We were on our way when we saw the message from Alhena to bring new weapons, so we had to go back. We used Molly Merle's portal to get here quicker.'

He and the other gnomes proceeded to measure up the humans for size, and then matched them with the appropriate swords and armour. Soon, everyone was well equipped and ready for battle. Merlin, who was now feeling a little better, got to his feet. Riding Charger, Morien led his army out to the front of the castle. They were met with the terrifying sight of Morgana's lava dragon crouching on the lawn, its flaming wings spread out, shielding the cursed statues that were lined up beside it. Sailing above the castle on the battle dragon was Morgana herself. When she saw that her stone trophies had been set free, she flew into a rage.

'I will finish you once and for all, girl.' She screamed at Mia.

'It wasn't *just* me!' trembled Mia, her legs nearly giving way to fear. 'Where is Tarask?' she whispered to Morien, but he did not hear.

Morgana flew to the edge of the battlefield where she hovered above her greatest prize, King Arthur. He had been placed in full moonlight, where all could witness her unyielding power over Camelot. The witch's eyes widened with triumph when she saw the broken spirits of her enemies. Mia heard a mass mumbling as her comrades began to lose confidence, but there was no time for anyone to turn back now, as with a swish of her wand, Morgana set her soldiers moving.

The mounted knights moved faster now, galloping forward on their stone horses, and swinging their maces above their heads. Morien rode out to meet

them, and one by one, smashed their weapons apart
with the flame sword. When the cursed kings and
queens marched forward, Mia and the others ran out
to help, each taking on one of the deadly statues.
Mia's training with Morien served her well and she
managed to disarm several of the slow statues with
her sword. But what they lacked in speed, they made
up for in strength, and the statues began knocking the
humans and gnomes to the ground with their stony
fists.

'Drive them into the moat,' shouted Morien,
seeing his untrained army being defeated. 'But do not
harm them, as they will carry their injuries when they
are freed.'

Mia and the others followed Morien's orders and
ran into the dried-up moat. The statues followed them,
and as Morien had planned, when they stepped over
the edge, they fell down the deep slope and became
trapped inside.

Merlin, now feeling stronger, and with his own
personal score to settle, came out from the trees.
Morgana was alarmed to see him alive. He was the

one person in Camelot who could defeat her, and she was certain that she had crushed him under the castle wall. With a note of hysteria in her voice, she commanded the lava dragon to rise. It exhaled a spray of fiery rocks over Merlin, sending everyone running for cover. Untouched by the flames, Merlin stayed where he was, and fixed his gaze firmly on the demonic creature. His eyes turned pale blue as he began to chant.

'Ignis in glacier vertere,' he said over and over.

As he did so, the oozing rivers of lava running across the dragon's body began to slow down. And as the lava slowed, so did the creature itself. Then the fire gradually turned to ice, and within a few seconds, the magical lava dragon had frozen to the spot. Morgana screamed as the wizard delivered a final set of words, and the ice dragon shattered into a million pieces.

Merlin then turned his attention to the witch, raising his staff in her direction. Morgana yanked on the battle dragon's reins and fled to the roof of the castle. Merlin, feeling too unsteady on his feet to follow her, turned to Mia and Morien, and said, 'I'm afraid it is up to you two now.'

Mia, dismissing all fear from her mind, stood upright and reached out her hand towards Morien. 'It is time,' she said. 'Give me the flame sword. I may be no match for an army of cursed statues, but I *can* break Morgana's spells.'

Morien grinned. 'I thought that you had lost your nerve,' he said, handing her the weapon. 'I'll make a knight of you yet.'

As soon as Mia's hand touched the handle of the flame sword it began to glow, and a great rush of energy filled her body. She suddenly felt invincible.

'Wow! What happened there?' she said.

'I told you that you have great power here,' replied Morien. 'The flame sword obviously feels it too.'

'Have courage, my friend,' said Merlin. 'The fate of Camelot now sits in your hands.' They both nodded encouragingly, and Mia nodded back. Then she ran off towards the castle.

# 15

## FAREWELL CAMELOT

*When you believe in good things, you can make them come true.*
*Just search in your heart, and you'll know what to do.*


What am I doing? thought Mia, as she ran up the spiral stairs of the tower. She realised that she actually had no idea, and that she would have to make a plan when she got to the top. Being alone was frightening, and she became even more anxious thinking about what Morgana would do to her when they finally came face to face. When she reached the roof, Mia pushed open the wooden door a few inches and peeked through the gap. There was no sign of Morgana, but a rotten fishy smell confirmed that she was nearby. She pushed the door a little further, and immediately jumped back. There, perched on the outer wall of the tower, was the battle dragon. Mia could not believe its size. It was the height of an elephant at least, and likely just as wide. Its copper scales were layered one on top of the other, like armoured tiles, sitting around the long spines that covered its neck and head.

On its back sat the witch, looking even more hideous up close. The ends of her long, ragged hair floated upwards like coral, and her moth-eaten cloak blew behind her like the sails of a ship. Mia shivered and was grateful that the witch was too distracted by what was happening below to notice her. She gripped the flame sword tightly, waiting for an opportunity to strike, but then, unexpectedly, Tarask's face appeared over the ledge. His yellow eyes drifted silently around the tower, sneaking up on Morgana unseen. The battle dragon sensed his presence and swung round, grabbing Tarask with its enormous claws. Tarask bit and scratched the battle dragon in an attempt to break free, and a ferocious airborne fight began.

Back on the ground, Merlin had been biding his time, waiting for Mia to draw Morgana's attention away from him, and as soon as he saw the battle dragon take to the air, he held up his staff and brought the end crashing down to the floor. The earth began to tremble.

'Get down!' he shouted. Everyone dived to the floor.

The lawn began to swell up like an ocean wave, rising and dipping, over and over, sending all of the cursed statues on the lawn and in the moat, toppling over. Then he ordered the ground to calm, before conjuring a green ball of light in his hands. He rolled it along the ground, and it covered the statues in a magical, soothing blanket, which sent them to sleep.

'Alhena!' he shouted, but the dream faerie had already sprung into action, and was busy ringing her bell over the sleeping statues. Blinding lights and music filled the lawn as the stone prisons cracked and fell apart, releasing the kings, queens, dragons, gnomes and knights from their enchantment.

'Welcome back!' said Morien, pulling one of the liberated knights to his feet.

'You took your time didn't you, brother?' Lancelot replied, punching Morien playfully on the arm. The friends hugged each other, full of joy to be back together again. Lancelot grabbed his horse, and the two knights went to find their king.

Mia, unaware of the happenings below, was busy watching the colossal blows being exchanged above her head. Tarask's army of dragons had returned and were corkscrewing through the air in pursuit of Morgana.

With King Arthur and the royal household safely hidden in the forest, and under the watch of the knights, Morien ran towards the castle to find Mia. But before he reached it, Morgana raised her arms and conjured a second lava dragon. The demonic creature showered fiery rain onto the lawn, blocking Morien's path and forcing him back to the forest. Tarask recoiled when the lava dragon set its sights on him and began circling. Then Mia saw something that terrified her. The lava dragon opened its mouth and a stream of wooden torches were exhaled into the air. One by one they lit, and paraded around Tarask and the other dragons, nudging them with their flames. The dragons thrashed about, trying to avoid the scorching stings, and soon fled, leaving Tarask alone and helpless.

Taking advantage of Tarask's confused state, the battle dragon swiped him with its tail, knocking him unconscious and sending him plummeting to the ground. Mia cried out in horror. Morgana looked down and saw her standing on the roof. An evil smile spread across her face.

'This will finish you, foolish girl,' she laughed, ordering the lava dragon to turn on Mia. The dragon spat out a large fireball, which catapulted towards the tower. 

Mia ran to the door but it was jammed shut, and the lock was on the other side. Remembering that she was holding the flame sword, she spun around and pounded the fireball back towards the witch.

Morgana darted out of the way, but the flaming missile hit the lava dragon at great speed and blasted it into two halves. Mia saw that the supernatural creature was made entirely of flames, with nothing but magic holding it together, so she picked up a piece of rock from the floor, and with one last superhuman swing of the flame sword, she sent it flying through the remains of the lava dragon, and it exploded into pieces.

Morgana went wild with rage, and she discharged a volley of lethal spells on Mia, but the flame sword and dragon armour protected her from the blows. When a crazy bolt of lightning headed her way, Mia held up the flame sword and reflected the light into the eyes of the battle dragon, throwing it off balance and sending it tumbling. Morgana lost control of the beast and slipped from the saddle, just managing to grab the reins with her fingertips. While she dangled above the lawn, she saw the broken statues lying on the ground below. She began to chant once more, and as she did so, the stony shells began to crawl back together. Merlin sent up a spark and snapped the reins. Morgana fell from the sky. Free from the witch's grasp, the battle dragon flew away.

Instead of letting her hit the floor and die, Merlin broke Morgana's fall just above the ground. There she lay, suspended in mid-air, unable to move. Everyone cheered as the wizard confiscated her wand, and then took her voice so that she could never harm anyone again.

Nobody but Mia had seen Tarask fall, and nobody noticed his lifeless body lying on the floor by the castle.

Morgana's former prisoners marched her off to the tiled hall and locked her up.

'I will personally see to it that you are taken back to the Great Lake,' said Merlin, and that the veil around you is resealed. Your evil days are over, Morgana,' he said.

Mia used the flame sword to smash through the tower door, then ran down the stairs and out of the castle. She headed straight towards Tarask's body. The dragons and gnomes soon gathered around him, and wept at the sacrifice he had made. Morien, Merlin and the dream faerie joined them.

'He fought so bravely,' Mia sobbed.

Those who were wearing them, took off their hats, and everyone bowed their heads in prayer.

Meanwhile, high up in the Mystical Mountains, Molly Merle had been watching the events in Camelot unfold through her secret crystal well. When she saw Tarask lying on the floor, she picked up her wand and jumped into one of the portals. A moment later, she arrived at the castle.

'Goodness me!' she said, taking in all the destruction around her.

Next, she went over to Tarask, and without hesitation waved her wand towards the dried-up castle moat. Magical blue water instantly began to flow into it. Job fetched a bucket and collected some of the sparkling water, then Molly poured it over the dragon. Tarask's body suddenly began to glisten with blue sparkles, and then, in a breath-taking moment, his spirit rose up from his body. Next to him, appeared the ghostly white stag.

'He's come to take Tarask to his next life,' whispered Merlin.

'He looks at rest,' sniffed Gobha, trying not to sob. Gobha's father, who was among those freed from the curse, put his arm around his son to comfort him.

The stag bowed to Tarask, and the two of them bounded off towards the golden beams of the rising sun.

'Where are they going?' asked Mia.

'Merlin answered, 'The stag is taking him back to another moment in time… where he was happiest.'

Merlin could see that Mia was confused, so he explained.

'All of our happiest moments are kept, and stored away somewhere in time,' he said. 'Then, when it is our time to leave this soil, we simply choose which of them we want to go back to. We never really die. We just move to a different time and live it over again.'

'So, while we miss those who we have lost,' checked Mia, 'somewhere in time, they still have us? And we still have them?'

'That's right,' said Merlin, 'but we must wait until the white stag comes to lead us there, for only *he* knows where those moments are kept.'

This thought comforted Mia, knowing that somewhere, she was still with her family. Soon, the green forest dragons arrived to take Tarask's body home to the dragon realm. Those that stayed, scurried around, tending to everyone's wounds with an ointment of herbs. Molly Merle picked up some oak leaves from the floor and soaked them with magical well water to make soothing bandages.

'This will do the trick,' she said to Mia, placing the bandages on the barks of the burnt trees. The potion trickled down their trunks and into the soil. As soon as Stickney Pygott and the other trees felt the tingle of the potion on their roots, they began to wake up.

'Brrr! that's better,' said Stickney, shaking himself awake. He kicked off the charcoaled bark, and underneath he was as good as new. The other trees were just as healthy too, although a few wondered where their leaves had gone.

He blinked his large eyes at Mia and smiled. 'I do apologise,' he said. 'I think that I fell fast asleep. I hope that I didn't miss anything.'

Mia laughed out loud. She was so happy to see him alive and well. 'Don't worry, Stickney,' she said. You didn't miss a thing!'

The citizens of Camelot soon arrived at the castle to celebrate their newly found freedom, and the defeat of Morgana. King Arthur led a special service of thanks on the lawn for those who had saved Camelot, and everyone bowed down in gratitude. The dream faerie, noticing the first colours of daylight appearing in the sky, and realising that she had broken most of the dream faerie rules already, waved goodbye and floated back to the dream realm. The king looked thoughtfully up at his castle and sighed contentedly before making his way inside. The guard cats, who were back at their posts, lowered their heads and purred as he passed through the gate. The cats also bowed for the other monarchs who Morgana had kept prisoner for centuries. As each of them stepped onto the drawbridge, they disappeared back to their own time in history, where they lived out their lives as they were meant to.

Mia and Morien saw Job striding past them with a ladder tucked under his arm. He stopped briefly when he saw them, and stood cheerfully with his hands on his hips.

'There is much to do,' he beamed, studying the collapsed roof and walls. 'I had better get started.'

He nodded at them gratefully, and then followed the others into the castle. Mia was pleased that the caretaker was finally going back to the life that he loved. She watched the gnome folk busying themselves, collecting the final wisps of Morgana's magic, and tossing them into the paddles of a giant portable mill wheel, which dragged and buried them deep underground. She casually looked towards Jack and Jiminy at the gatehouse, and something puzzled her.

'If Morgana is still alive, why are the guard cats letting King Arthur and the others back into the castle?' she remarked to Morien. 'I thought that they were loyal to her.'

'I have no idea,' replied Morien. 'Cats can be changeable creatures.'

Then something dawned on her, and she ran over to the gatehouse.

'It was *you,* wasn't it?' she said to the cats. '*You* opened the sealed tunnel in the moat for me!'

Jack and Jim stayed silent, and looked as disinterested as ever.

'You *wanted* me to find Morien's letter.'

She turned to Morien, who had joined them. 'They weren't protecting Morgana by not letting us into the castle before,' she said. 'They were protecting *us* from *her*!'

The cats purred, and their eyes slowly closed.

'And I suspect that you deliberately let us find Morgana's spell book, didn't you?' added Morien.

The guard cats nudged him with their heads, and let him pat their noses.

'So, I didn't have the power to break Morgana's spells after all,' muttered Mia, feeling rather disappointed.

'Of course you did,' came a voice from behind. It was Merlin.

'The flame sword only gives its power to those who believe in it, and themselves. While you held it, you believed that you could beat Morgana, and so you *did*. Those who truly believe, can do anything… can't they Jack.' Merlin softly patted Jack on the head, adding, 'The guard cats just helped you to find that belief.'

He bid Mia farewell and went inside to rest. Later that day he would be making the long journey to the Great Lake with Morgana, and he would need his wits about him.

Mia and Sir Morien sat down and watched the red sky over the castle turn to blue, as the new day arrived.

'I suppose that I should be going home too,' said Mia, looking towards the forest.

'Can you not stay?' asked Morien.

Mia slowly shook her head.

'My own world is in need of healing too,' she said. 'Now that I have the courage, I shall look for my own quest there.'

'I understand,' he said. 'We owe you a great debt, Mia. I will never forget you.'

'And I will make sure that my world doesn't forget you either,' she replied.

She wiped a tear from her eye, took one last look around her, and then went to find the magic oak tree.

'I'm ready to go home now, Stickney,' she said, waking him.

Stickney Pygott looked at her sleepily and nodded. Then he yawned, and as he exhaled, brilliant shards of white light exploded from his trunk. The magic doorway opened. Mia stepped inside and found the leafy staircase waiting for her. With a giant leap, Stickney ripped his long roots from the soil and took to the sky. They flew over the castle and saw Morien and the others up on the roof, waving them goodbye. Mia waved back, feeling sad to be leaving Camelot and the friends that she had made.

She took one last look behind her and could hardly believe her eyes. The white stag and Tarask were flying next to them, and they had the twilight travellers with them. The old man, the children, and all the others who were trapped in Tarask's lair were finally going home.

'He went back and freed them!' she cried, whooping with happiness, but Stickney was not listening, he was busy looking out for those ill-mannered mountain dragons.

It was still early in the morning when they landed back on the playing field behind Mia's house. She smiled when she heard Cairo barking, remembering how Mr Oliver had a time travelling secret too. How much more they would have to talk about now, she thought.

As she walked down the leafy staircase, she noticed Sir Morien's old book lying on the floor. She picked it up and opened it. The pages were no longer blank, they were now filled with countless stories about his adventures at Camelot.

'You will not be forgotten,' she said, looking at his picture. And later that day, just as she had promised, Mia took the book to the town library and left it on the history shelf for everyone to read.

© www.magical-storybook.com